Coming for him . . .

He swung around, peering into the fog. Because of the clouds swirling and shifting around him, he couldn't tell where the sound of shuffling feet was coming from.

But it was coming, coming for him.

Suddenly the monster leaped out of the gray void and grabbed him.

Falling to the ground, David grasped it and rolled. The hairy arms were strong as steel bands wrapping around his chest. A snarl from its snout carried a fetid breath. The stench of a decaying carcass, the heat of anger and evil. . . .

Terrifying thrillers by Diane Hoh:

Funhouse

The Accident

The Invitation

The Train

The Fever

Nightmare Hall: The Silent Scream

Nightmare Hall: The Roommate

Nightmare Hall: Deadly Attraction

Nightmare Hall: The Wish

Nightmare Hall: The Scream Team

Nightmare Hall: Guilty

Nightmare Hall: Pretty Please

Nightmare Hall: The Experiment

Nightmare Hall: The Night Walker

Nightmare Hall: Sorority Sister

Nightmare Hall: Last Date

Nightmare Hall: The Whisperer

Nightmare Hall: Monster

NIGHTMARE HALL

Monster

DIANE HOH

SCHOLASTIC INC.
New York Toronto London Auckland Sydney

No part of this publication may be reproduced in whole or in part, or stored in a retrieval system, or transmitted in any form or by any means, electronic, mechanical, photocopying, recording, or otherwise, without written permission of the publisher. For information regarding permission, write to Scholastic Inc., 555 Broadway, New York, NY 10012.

ISBN 0-590-48321-8

12 11 10 9 8 7 6 5 4 3 2   4 5 6 7 8 9/9

Printed in the U.S.A.   01

First Scholastic printing, July 1994

Prologue

A soft rustling sound broke the silence around Varsity Pond. The couple sitting on the park bench, enjoying the soft spring night, thought nothing of it. An owl, left homeless when the old Peabody gym had burned, had moved into a hollow oak tree near the pond. Bird-watchers from the Biology I class kept an eye on the tree, hoping the bird was nesting.

The girl snuggled close as the guy she was with stroked her hair with gentle hands. His first kiss was soft, lingering.

A groan from behind them caused her to pull back, alarmed. A musty smell grew stronger, became rotten, like a skunk long dead.

The low growl sent shivers throughout the girl's body. Her chest squeezed, leaving her struggling to breathe. She wanted to scream, but no sound left her open mouth.

Before she could get to her feet, before they

could run, the beast roared, attacked, slashing out with long, razor-sharp claws.

Everyone had joked about the monster stalking students on the campus of Salem University. Everyone thought it was a prank by the Sigma Chis.

The couple could testify that the creature was no prank.

They had evidence that the creature was real.

They could put the rumors to rest.

If they lived.

Chapter 1

"College is for geniuses," Abby McDonald announced to the friends walking to the library with her.

"Are you still behind?" Jerry Todd teased. "You had all of spring break to catch up."

"Believe me, she spent it studying, too." David Waters grimaced, but he put his arm around Abby's waist and squeezed.

Abby couldn't believe that David was still speaking to her. She had been a total drag lately, turning down all of his great ideas for dates and parties. He had even invited her to go to Florida over break, courtesy of his parents' generosity, and she'd had to say no. After four years of going out with Abby, he should be used to it. Maybe he was. Or tired of it? Maybe he was that, too.

"How can it have been only two weeks since classes started again?" Abby moaned. "I have a history paper to write, a book to read for my English class, and that dumb lab project to do for my intro chem class. I'll never keep up."

"You mean you might not make straight A's." David smiled. "Would the world come to an end?"

Abby winced but said, "No, but my scholarship might. And without that money, I'd have to drop out and work in the cafeteria full-time instead of part-time. And my parents would kill me."

"Now we get to the real worry," David said. "They're too hard on you, Abby."

Gina Putnam shook her head. "You did this to yourself, Abby. You're taking chemistry, a lit course — where everyone knows you have to read a million books — American history, freshman comp, *and* working part-time? Give yourself a break. Nobody could keep up with that load their first year in college. Or even their fourth year. Have you never heard of easy classes? Like drama? Or communications?" Gina pretended to faint. "I'm going to be a movie star, make a ton of money, and let someone else mix my chemicals." She started tickling Jerry and he turned on her. Both of them ran ahead laughing.

"Children." David smiled. "Want me to wait for you until the library closes, Abby?" They had just reached the huge building. David brushed back the dark hair that kept falling over his forehead.

"Thanks, David, but I'm going from here to the chem lab. Doctor Curruthers said Griswold Hall would be open and if I could find the janitor he'd let me into the lab."

"When are you going to sleep, Abby?" David looked truly worried. "You'll make yourself sick, and then you really won't keep up." David had the most handsome face. Abby hated to see it marred with a frown.

She reached out and touched his smooth cheek. "What else can I do? I'll get used to the pace. I'm sure I will. College is just so different from high school, and classes are so much harder."

"So is spending time with you." David leaned over and planted a quick kiss on her lips. The gesture said one thing. His tone of voice said another.

Abby felt heavy inside, and it wasn't all due to staying up late studying. David was getting impatient with her. If she didn't find some time for him, he'd find another girlfriend. They had been going together since they were sophomores in high school. She was thrilled when he decided to come to Salem University with her. Who else would put up with me, she thought.

I know I'm too serious. I know I study too much.

She sighed. She just didn't have time to worry about David. She glanced around, found a free seat, and hurried to the shelves.

By the time she'd finished writing her paper, the library was a half hour from closing. She was almost the only student left. No one else was working this hard. But at least she'd finished.

She turned to stand up with her load of books and the top one started to slide. Before she could grab it, she spilled everything in a noisy avalanche. "Oh." She slumped in the hard, uncomfortable library chair and wished she could curl up right there and sleep.

Spinning around, she found herself looking down on a head of curly, dark red hair. "Oh, you don't have to do that."

"I don't mind," he said, looking up at her with a gorgeous smile.

"You're a lot nicer than most guys, then," she told him.

"I'm not most guys." His blue eyes twinkled.

He sure wasn't. And he wasn't a freshman either. Wouldn't Gina faint for real if she saw boring, studious Abby with an upperclassman on her arm?

What was she doing? Just a few hours ago

she'd been worrying about David getting tired of her. Now she was flirting with another guy.

"Thanks," she said, flipping her reddish blonde hair over her shoulder and taking the load of books he handed her. "Abby McDonald, natural-born klutz." She slid a few fingers out from under the books.

"Careful." He laughed and squeezed her hand but pushed it back under her notebook. "I sort of guessed you were from a long line of Irish lassies. Martin Beecher, at your service."

"Well, thanks a lot, Martin Beecher. Now I have to run." Suddenly she felt her face heating up and her tongue getting numb. She didn't want to say something stupid.

She set a fast pace out of the library. But as she crossed the grassy commons, something made her look around. He stood on the library steps, watching her. She jerked her head around and hurried on. Maybe studying makes a girl beautiful. If that was the case, she should be drop-dead gorgeous by now.

Within minutes of leaving the lights of the library, she wished she'd told David to wait for her and walk her to Griswold Hall, the science building. Or that Martin Beecher would have said, "I just happen to be going your way."

Maybe it was too late to work on her project after all. The campus was completely deserted.

And she didn't remember it having so many trees. Or being so dark once you left the main sidewalks.

Griswold Hall snuggled into a pocket of land beside a small lake, really a pond, called Varsity Pond. The closer she got to the water, the deeper the shadows seemed. To her left something rustled in the bushes. Wings fluttered and a dark shape swooped past her, raising the hair on the back of her neck.

That was an owl, Abby McDonald. Have you never seen an owl before? No, she didn't think she had. And she had certainly never heard the sharp squeak that abruptly stopped the rustling.

Now she heard footsteps behind her.

Slowly she twisted her head, the same way she imagined the owl moving. Her body kept going forward.

There was no one behind her. Her own steps echoed through the thick night air.

She ran the last few feet to Griswold, drawn like a moth to the lights glowing on either side of the door. She yanked open the door, clutching her books in front of her as if the heavy volumes would protect her. Protect her? From what? Her imagination?

Inside, the silent front hall was almost as scary as outside in the darkness. There was a dim light, but the hall gave off hollow echoes as she walked up the stairs and towards the lab. Doesn't anyone else study at night at Salem University?

"Oh!" She jumped back as a tall, slim man came around a corner towards her. Dressed in overalls, he carried a mop. His long face held a scowl as if he hated his job.

"Are you the custodian?" she asked. "Doctor Curruthers said you'd open the chem lab for me. I have to finish a project."

He stared at her until her knees wobbled. Had no one ever come here at night to work? Finally he turned and walked towards the lab door. Taking out a huge ring with dozens of jingling keys, he selected one carefully, turned it in the door with a click.

"Pull it shut when you leave. It'll lock itself." He hurried away.

"Yessir," she whispered, sliding into the lab.

The door creaked and banged closed behind her. Strong chemical smells filled her nostrils. Yep, this was the chem lab. She froze, leaning on the cool door for a moment. Then she headed for her table.

"What are you doing here?" a voice growled from one dim corner.

Abby jumped. Her books slid away again with a whoosh and a crash. Great.

And of all people to be here, after her wishing someone — anyone — would show up, the class creep makes an appearance.

Stan Hurley looked like a comic book version of a mad scientist. Or a young, disturbed Albert Einstein. His hair was a peculiar shade of blond and was steel-wool curly. Jerry had dubbed him Professor Brillo Pad their first day of class.

She wished Jerry were here now, making her laugh.

Word was he really was a genius — Stan, not Jerry — and one of her classmates had whispered that some people thought he was just a little bit crazy. Over the first three months of the semester, she'd heard several strange stories about him.

He was short but looked as if he lifted weights in secret. He was certainly no ninety-pound weakling. He wore those glasses with no rims. Now, with a white lab coat on, she waited for him to say, "Since you're here, come see this body I'm sewing together with spare parts I dug this evening from the cemetery."

What was he doing? Abby set her books down and moved towards him. As long as they were going to be here together, she'd try to be friendly.

"What's that weird brew you're cooking up,

Stan?" Abby reached for his notes. "It smells awful."

"None of your business!" Stan snatched up all his notes and stuffed them into his notebook. "What are you doing here at night?"

"I could ask the same thing of you. I came to work on my extra-credit project. Dr. Curruthers said it was okay. Does he know you come here at night and mess with those chemicals?" Abby could be nasty if she felt like it.

"I have a key." Stan continued putting his work away.

"Oh." Abby moved back to her table. A lot more questions ran through her mind. Does Prof. C. know you have a key? Who gave it to you? Did you pour wax in the keyhole and make it yourself? She heard the door slam and was glad when he had gone — for a few minutes. Then she began to wonder why couldn't he keep working with her there? She had to admit she preferred to be here with him rather than all alone.

Abby concentrated on her experiment. She finally got the Bunsen burner lighted — Gina often did that for her, since Abby was a bit afraid of the thing — and had heated one test tube, when she heard a click at the door. She looked up, but no one entered.

Reaching for a beaker, she paused. Should she mix these two before or after she heated the test tube? She couldn't remember what she'd planned. With her elbow she tried to turn the page in her notebook.

The lab door opened. She dropped the beaker at the same time she bumped the test tube. Maybe she hadn't gotten the holder tight, maybe it burst from the heat. Whatever, the whole mess splashed across the floor at her feet.

"Oh, no. Not just as I was finished." Abby couldn't have felt more disappointed. All that work.

She glared at the janitor who stood at the door. He didn't say a word, just peeked in, shook his head as if to say I'm not paid to clean up after you. He let the door swing closed by itself.

Grabbing some paper towels from over the sink, she ran back to mop up the mess she'd made. It smelled awful, almost as bad as that stuff Stan was mixing. The fumes stung her nostrils. She coughed, laughed — what else could she do? She tossed the whole experiment into the wastebasket. No, she changed her mind. Better not.

Quickly she moved into the bathroom attached to the lab. The one with the shower where they'd get scrubbed down if they spilled something caustic. She dumped the whole mess into the toilet and flushed.

"I give up," she quipped, waving good-bye to an hour's work.

"I hope so. What are you doing?" A voice behind her said.

She jumped and dropped the wastebasket. The metal can crashed and clattered, echoing through the empty lab.

"Oh, David, you scared me. Ms. Klutz strikes again. I was almost through when I dropped the whole mess."

"Give it up, Abby. You're too tired to be working here. Jerry and Gina are outside. We came out for you. And because Vinnie's is calling us. You'll feel a whole lot better after a double cheese and pepperoni with olives and mushrooms."

"I'll feel a whole lot better when the summer comes. But you're right. This night is finished. I'll try to do this over tomorrow." Abby gladly picked up her books. With her free hand she grabbed David's arm and pulled him close. "Want to know who was here when I came in? Acting weird as usual?"

Abby laughed as they dashed out of the silent, creepy building and tumbled into the backseat of Gina's car. Thank goodness for friends to remind her of the important things in life.

Chapter 2

The next morning Abby paid for her late night — *another* late night. She'd gotten very little sleep since she came to college, it seemed. She thought college was supposed to be fun. So why was she so worn out — exhausted in the morning, frantic by day, desperately trying to keep up?

As she sat on her bed, trying to shake off the heavy, soggy weight of her body and pull herself to her feet, she finally noticed that her roommate's bed hadn't been slept in — again.

Why didn't Carrie Milholland have to study? And where did she go every night? Abby hadn't gotten to know her very well. Her first semester roommate had dropped out, and Carrie had entered school in January. Abby had liked Carrie the few times they'd talked. She thought they might be able to be close friends.

But Carrie seemed to be with her boyfriend most of the time.

"May you flunk out your first year," Abby said, venting her frustration on someone who couldn't vent back.

Dragging herself into the shower, she stood under cold water until her brain was shocked into a low level of function. It was better than nothing.

Gina waited for her on the front steps of the Quad. "Oh, Abby, why did we stay out so late last night? Don't ever let me do that again."

"*Let* you? You and David and Jerry lured *me* away. It's not my fault."

"Someone in this foursome has to have some discipline. You seem best suited for that job."

"Do you really think I'm a disciplined drudge, Gina? Is that what everyone thinks?" Abby groaned. She wanted people to think she was *fun*, not "disciplined." But she had to study a lot to maintain her scholarship. How could she balance out the two?

"Yes, Abby, you're a drudge, but we love you anyway." Gina laughed, her eyes squeezing shut. "Actually I admire your discipline. I just can't do it."

"Have you ever tried?" Abby smiled at Gina. With her short-short hair, her heart-shaped face, and those crinkly eyes, she looked like a mischievous pixie.

"No."

They entered the dining hall arm in arm, still laughing.

"So, you've heard the news." Jerry's face registered exaggerated disappointment. "I wanted to be the one to tell you."

"What news?" Gina took the tray Jerry handed her as they got in line. "We're having *huevos rancheros* with hot, hot salsa for breakfast at last?" Gina had come to Salem University from Texas, and apparently they didn't eat like normal people down there.

"Do you really eat that chili pepper stuff for breakfast, Gina?" asked Abby. "My stomach would turn somersaults all day."

"Yes. It lights a fire that gives you energy all day."

"I'll light your fire, Tex," Jerry said, "but it may not last all day. You'll have to meet me again after second period and then at noon and then — "

"Dream on, Romeo. So if a real breakfast isn't the news, what is?"

"Apparently there's a monster loose on campus." David spoke for the first time, other than a nod and a hug for Abby. There were dark circles under his eyes as if he'd stayed up even later than their pizza rendezvous.

Abby burst out laughing. "You've got to be kidding. A monster — like Frankenstein's? Or *Alien?*"

"Or like that monster in *Forbidden Planet*. Boy, that was a great movie." Jerry was practically drooling and rubbing his hands together. "Or the original version of *The Thing*. The remake was a disaster. That gooey glob wasn't scary at all."

"Everyone in my end of the dorm was talking about strange noises down near the Sigma Chi house behind the pond." David heaped his plate with hash browns and then took three pieces of buttered toast. He was always carbo loading for tennis practice.

"Well, that's easily explained." Gina shook her head. "Probably some of those fraternity animals skinny-dipping in the dark."

"I'll bet it's some kind of prank." After talking about monster breakfasts Abby settled for toast and black coffee. "You know, hazing or trying to scare the girls at the Omega house on that same block."

"Here comes Sissy King," Gina said, waving at a girl with long dark hair and about a pound of skillfully applied makeup on her face. "Let's get her to sit with us. She always knows all the gossip."

Sissy didn't need encouragement. She slid into a chair on the other side of David and smiled at him. Her nearly black eyes sparkled and flirted. "David, hi. Did you get your sociology paper finished?"

What sociology paper? Abby wondered. David never mentioned he had a paper due, but Sissy seemed to know all about it. Abby and David had tried to get all their classes together, but ended up with only chemistry. David could pass chemistry just by showing up in class. Why hadn't she asked him to help her last night? She wouldn't have spoiled her project, and she'd have time for him now.

Because you like being independent, Abby, a little voice inside her reminded. Because you hate clinging-vine girls like Sissy.

"What do you think about the monster on campus?" Abby asked, moving closer to David and leaning around him. Maybe Sissy hadn't noticed that David was taken. Abby would remind her.

"I love it. The drama department's next play is a creepy thriller. I'll bet someone is practicing for tryouts. I don't need to practice, since I had a lot of starring roles in high school." Sissy twisted a curl about her forefinger. "But Ms. Alexander may not want to give big roles to freshmen." She pulled her mouth into a pout and stared at David.

Gina caught Abby's eye and made a face, wiggling her shoulders like Sissy. Abby bit her lip to keep from giggling.

"You know, you guys can laugh all you like, but I think there really could be things on our planet we don't know about." Jerry pointed a knife dripping with strawberry jam at David and Sissy, then smeared it on an English muffin. "I vill make believers of you all." He hunched his shoulders and narrowed his eyes. "I vill make you vish you had listened to me and stayed inside at night."

They all laughed at Jerry's antics, but Abby felt her stomach lurch. Maybe something really had followed her last night. Maybe she had just missed seeing what everyone was talking about.

"Don't all stare at once," Sissy leaned in and spoke in a dramatic whisper. "But the evil scientist Stan Hurley is going to sit right behind us. He's probably scoping out his next victim."

David didn't get silly often, but he joined in. Maybe he was showing off for Sissy. He whispered, too. "We're safe. He would only want Abby's brain. Geniuses only attract geniuses."

She was probably being extra sensitive because of Sissy, but David's remark made Abby have to breathe deeply and squeeze her eyes shut. Suddenly tears wanted to spill over. She covered with her own joke.

"I thought only opposites attract. Isn't that a scientific law?"

Gina pulled Abby out of her sudden funk. "So he'd want me?" She made her face so woeful, Abby giggled, then laughed out loud.

"Maybe," Jerry said, "just maybe he has zee formula for zee salsa dip. Hey, Stan." He was actually going to speak to Stan Hurley.

Stan looked surprised that anyone would call his name. He had been shuffling through some papers while he ate.

"You got zee extra-spicy salsa dip?" Jerry stood up as if to go get it if Stan said yes.

The look Stan gave them was evil enough to turn them all to stone. He returned to shuffling his papers, then opened a book.

"I just love a guy with a sense of humor, don't you, Gina?" Jerry sat back down and kept talking. "You'll be very happy together."

Gina was practically under the table from laughing.

Abby continued to smile, but inside she shivered. Stan was now staring at her as if it were her idea to tease him.

She stood, balancing her tray in one hand,

her book bag in the other. "I've got a nine o'clock class, guys. I'm going to be late."

"See you later." David waved, then turned back to talk to Sissy. But Abby was distracted before she had time to worry about David.

Stan Hurley had picked up his own tray and was following her.

"Excuse me. Excuse me." She bumped three people out of the way, slammed her tray into the revolving section of wall that would move it into the kitchen.

Then she pushed through the crowd that headed for the door and their own classes. Glancing back, she saw Stan was still staring at her.

Outside, she bounced down the steps and ran, actually *ran*, to the English building.

Chapter 3

Lenny Latham wondered why he ever thought he wanted to be a member of Sigma Chi. Hazing was silly. Fraternities were silly — un-American. Maybe he'd feel differently tomorrow. If he got through this night.

He didn't like being outside alone at night. But Foster Tuttle knew that. They'd been in the same Boy Scout troop, even though Foster was two years older. They'd been camping together. And Foster had done everything he could think of to make Lenny miserable. Here he was doing it again.

Lenny's last initiation task was to stay all night, alone, on the grounds of the old Peabody Gym. Everyone knew the old gym was haunted. And even though it had burned down, everyone said the ghost hadn't left. Now it was haunting the ruins.

To top it off, he knew it was Sigma Chi,

maybe led by Foster, who had started the rumor about a monster on campus. Everyone was talking about it.

Silly. There were no such things as monsters, werewolves, vampires.

Or were there?

Lenny looked around. The skeletal remains of the gym rose up around him like gray tombstones or some sort of ritual stones. Not unlike the photos of Stonehenge he had seen in books.

There was no moon tonight, making the campus even darker than usual. It wasn't that late, but no one would be hanging around down here. So it was quiet. Too quiet. And cold. Too cold for this late in the spring. At least it wasn't raining.

He pulled his sleeping bag around him. He was letting his imagination run away. Just go to sleep, he commanded his brain. Just stop thinking, his brain shouted back.

He closed his eyes, but then he heard every tiny sound. A slight rustle of limbs at the back of the gym's shell. The trees were dead, black statues reaching bony arms to the night, but also scraping the blackened stone pillars.

A murmur of wings, probably an owl. Or some other night bird hunting? What kind of birds searched for food at night?

Aren't you hungry, Lenny?

Food. His own stomach rumbled. Why hadn't he brought a huge supply of chips, some sandwiches, a thermos of hot chocolate? Nourishment. If he wasn't going to sleep he could eat. Why hadn't he brought a book? He could have used his flashlight to read all night.

Next there was the sound of footsteps. Footsteps? He sat up again and listened. Nothing. His imagination again.

Okay, he'd go to the bathroom. Even though it meant getting out of the sleeping bag. He had all his clothes on. Just in case he had to make a quick getaway.

Getaway from what?

He pulled himself out of the snug bag with the rustle of parachute silk, or whatever this bag was made of. He'd borrowed it, since his was old and not very comfortable. Slipping on his running shoes, he stood up and walked away from the nest he'd made.

What he fully expected was some of the frat members to show up. Try to scare him. He heard footsteps again. There they were, earlier than he'd expected. The luminous hands on his watch face read eleven-thirty.

"Foster, is that you? Come on in and have a cup of cocoa." He'd pretend he had some. "I can use some company."

No answer. He didn't expect one. But the

footsteps grew louder. The steps were heavy, dragging. Pour it on, Foster. I'm ready for you now. I'm not even scared. Much.

Lenny turned and headed back to his bag. A gasping, panting sound came from the shadows of one crumbling wall of the gym. Pretty good. Great sound. Authentic.

He waited until they were close. So close he could smell the garlic and moldy socks they were using so he'd know they were coming. Don't spoil their trick, he thought. When he couldn't stand the suspense anymore, he grasped the black rubber tube of his flashlight more firmly and slid the ON button forward.

The beam spotlighted a huge hulk. It hunched forward, curling short arms in front of its chest. It kept shuffling towards Lenny. Long nails reached for him.

His feet froze in his size eleven Reeboks. His heart thudded until he could feel it throbbing in his temples. He tried to speak, tried to shout, "No! No!"

He raised both hands to ward off the beast. With a snarl the monster attacked, threw him to the ground, raked his face. He felt the welts sting. Blood ran freely down his face.

That was the last thing he remembered.

* * *

"What did I tell you? What did I tell you, Abby?" Abby and Gina found Jerry and David waiting outside the Quad Caf the next day. Sissy was with them. Abby noticed that Sissy moved back a step from David when Abby appeared.

Sissy lived in the same dorm with David and Jerry, Devereaux Hall. More and more Abby wanted to scream at her mother for being so conservative. Abby's mother had been adamant about Abby being in the all-women's dorm for a year. "By then you'll be used to the freedom of college, Abby," her mother had said. "Then I can't protect you anymore."

Abby couldn't help but wonder what Sissy's mother was like. Had Mrs. King ever tried to teach Sissy any social graces? Like, one does not steal a friend's guy. Then again, was Abby *friends* with Sissy? Yes, reluctantly, since Sissy had attached herself more and more to their crowd.

Abby gave her attention to Jerry's question. "I don't know, Jerry. What did you tell me? Am I supposed to remember all the gibberish you come up with?" She smiled, grateful to Jerry for keeping them all from being too serious. For keeping them sane when they were all under pressure from tough classes.

"I told you that monsters really existed. I

have the biggest collection of monster comics and movies of anyone in my hometown, but I've never seen a real one. I wish I could."

"Careful what you wish for, Jerry," said Sissy. "You might get your wish."

"Lenny Latham wasn't hurt badly. Mainly just scared. At first he thought the monster was a frat joke. But then it attacked him."

"He wasn't hurt?" asked Gina.

"Just scratched up some. And he banged his head when he fainted. He has a slight concussion."

"Wait, guys," Abby protested as they went into the cafeteria. "You mean someone saw this rumored monster? It's *real*?"

David smiled at Abby. She wanted to grab him and hug him. He never said much in the morning, but he sure was cute. "He not only saw it, but it attacked him," David said.

"The Sigma Chis made him stay overnight in the ruins of the old Peabody Gym." Sissy said. "You know the one that's haunted, except now that the gym burned, the ghost haunts the ruins. When the monster first appeared, he figured it was one of the upperclassmen dressed up. But it was *real*!" Sissy laughed and scrunched up her shoulders. "Isn't that super-scary-*awesome*? Let's go over to the ruins tonight and see if we can find it. We'll be safe if we stick together." She was inviting everyone, but Sissy looked only at David.

"I don't think I want to." Gina took a tray and started looking over the breakfast selections.

"You scared?" Jerry asked. "I'll protect you."

"Oh, that relieves my mind considerably." Gina took a deep breath and pretended to relax all over. "I'll have a ninety-pound weakling for a bodyguard."

"Do you have any Wheaties?" Jerry called to the girl behind the counter. "The Breakfast of Champions? And ninety-pound weaklings?"

Greta Lyons smiled, knowing he was teasing. "Sorry, Jerry. All out. Hi, Abby. Can you work for me this weekend? I need to go back home."

"I think so, Greta." Abby could use some extra hours, even though she had planned to study all weekend. She was almost caught up. Of course, some teacher would probably spoil that by giving them another paper to write or extra reading. "I sure don't have time to go home until the semester is over."

Every table in the Quad Caf buzzed with last night's events. Abby overheard snatches of conversation as she looked for an empty space.

"Monster attack." "Furry." "Long claws.

You should see Lenny's face." "Terrible smell, like sewer water mixed with garlic."

"I thought monsters were afraid of garlic," Abby said. "I just heard someone say this thing smells like garlic."

Jerry loved showing off his expertise. "Well, vampires don't like garlic. And werewolves hate nearly the same stuff as vampires. But I'm not sure there's anything that will repel a monster. There are so many different kinds."

"Ohhh, I love it." Sissy squealed. "I'm going to need protection on the campus at night. Any volunteers?" She didn't look at David, but since she sat beside him, he was the one she leaned on.

"There comes Stan Hurley, Sissy." Jerry stood up. "I'll go ask him if he's busy."

"Don't you dare." Sissy's dark eyes shot daggers at Jerry. "I wouldn't be caught dead with that weirdo."

Jerry hummed creepy music. "You may get *your* wish, Sissy-babe. First he'll drug you with one of those awful potions he mixes in the chem lab. Then he'll murder you in his monster-den. You will truly be caught dead with him."

"You think he could be involved in what's happening?" Gina asked. "If we're going to take this seriously, there must be someone behind the stunt."

Abby stared at Stan. She was glad he'd sat with his back to them. She had never found out what he wanted the other morning when he'd followed her. And she had caught him staring at her a couple of times since.

Now she felt someone else staring at her. Her eyes met those of Martin Beecher, the guy who'd picked up her books in the library. He smiled, then got up and left. Abby felt her face getting hot. How could she be in love with David, but attracted to another guy?

"Listen, it's Friday," Gina said, sipping her second cup of coffee. "I have an idea. Let's get together tonight and look for this thing. Like Sissy says, we'll be safe together. It'll be fun."

"Tell me where to meet you," Abby said. "I'm on clean-up at the cafeteria tonight, and then I have one more thing to finish in the chem lab. I started it yesterday, but I'm having trouble figuring it out."

"Abby, didn't you hear me? It's Friday. You sure are a party pooper." Gina pretended to pout.

"I've worked too hard this semester to blow it now." Abby insisted on meeting them. "Where will you be?"

"How about the Tower?" said Sissy. "We can see all over the campus with those telescopes."

"Hey, great idea." Jerry smiled at Abby. "You won't get involved with Hurley and forget to come, will you?"

Why did he have to say that? "If Stan Hurley is in the lab this evening, I'll finish my extra-credit project tomorrow."

"He'll be there. Covered with dust and cobwebs." Gina grinned. "I think he lives in the chem lab."

This time, Abby wished David would say he'd come help her finish her experiment. But he didn't. And she sure wasn't going to ask him for help. "Okay, I'll be there about nine."

"Be careful walking across the campus." David looked at her as she picked up her breakfast tray. He still didn't offer to come get her, though.

Then Sissy had to put in, "I'll take care of David till you get there."

I'll bet you will, Abby thought. She left for her early class, determined not to worry about Sissy or David. If he wanted an overly dramatic, clinging vine, he could have her.

But if Sissy didn't keep her hands to herself, Abby would tear her into bite-size pieces and feed her to the monster herself.

Chapter 4

Abby was exhausted when she finished cleaning up in the cafeteria. She wished she could just go back to the dorm and sleep for about twelve hours. The idea that her bed was only a couple of floors away nagged at her. How could she go to the lab and then out with David? A little voice inside her said, no wonder he's attracted to Sissy. She has a lot of energy and a lot of time to pay attention to him.

She sighed, grabbed her chem book and her notebook, and forced her heavy feet to climb the stairs and leave the Quad.

A lovely spring evening greeted her. The whole campus smelled of freshly mowed grass and lilacs. Friday evening — there were people everywhere, throwing Frisbees, sitting on the grass laughing and talking, just hanging out. Who would have had any idea that there was some kind of beast loose on campus?

Abby still had trouble accepting that there was. She still suspected that "the monster" was a Sigma Chi fraternity prank. She hadn't seen Lenny Latham's face. Everyone said it was scratched badly. But he could have fallen, trying to escape the guys who were teasing him. She knew Lenny. He was a world-class nerd. She wondered why Sigma Chi was pledging him. Maybe they just needed an underdog, someone to hassle or play tricks on.

The campus was much quieter near Griswold Hall, and shadows grew long around the pond she had to pass to get there. Despite her doubt about the existence of a supernatural beast, she still quickened her steps, glancing all around.

Once inside the building, her steps echoed off the high walls and up and down the stairwell. She would never get used to coming in here without swarms of students running up and down.

To her surprise, the lab wasn't locked. Maybe the janitor was tired of opening it for people. As predictable as Friday pop quizzes, Stan Hurley was huddled over a Bunsen burner in the back of the lab. Abby didn't even acknowledge that she'd seen him. Eyes straight ahead, she hurried to her table, took things from her drawer, and looked over her notes. Her eyes blurred.

Did she really need to do this — try it again? Yes, she did. Dr. Curruthers had announced that anyone who needed to pull up a sagging grade or assure an A could do extra-credit reports or experiments. He had suggested some, but told the class to be creative. "Just don't blow up the place," he warned with a laugh. Apparently someone had done that a few years back.

"Abby?" Stan spoke from behind, making her jump and almost drop a test tube.

"Oh, you scared me, Stan. Don't do that — don't sneak up on me."

"I didn't mean to scare you." He ran his fingers through his kinky curls. "I — I just thought we might get to be friends. I mean, since we both seem to be in here so much."

Oh, lord, was that why Stan Hurley had been staring at her? He liked her. What could she say?

"Well — I — I don't have a lot of extra time, Stan. And I do have a boyfriend. But thanks, Stan. That was nice of you to offer." Could she just say no to an offer of friendship? He hadn't asked for a date.

A little devil inside her almost made her giggle. She could see herself showing up at the Tower tonight with Stan Hurley. "Stan needs friends, you guys. He's picked us. How about it?"

Abby had hardly looked at Stan. Now she pretended to be really busy, keeping her eyes on her notebook and the red powder she was measuring and weighing.

She felt his presence, heavy and dark. She felt his need, his longing. *Don't touch me, Stan. Please don't touch me.*

Suddenly she felt his anger as he spun around and walked back to his table. Had she made a mistake? While she didn't want Stan for a friend, she didn't need him for an enemy, either.

She dumped what she had started into the wastebasket. She wouldn't work on her project after all. She needed to get out of the lab with its strange smells and dark corners.

"Good night," she said as she left, not even knowing why. The word wasn't an apology, but some gesture seemed polite. Stan didn't answer. She didn't expect him to.

Practically running down two flights of stairs, she pulled open the heavy front door, stepped out, leaned on it, and pulled in the fresh air. Why did she always feel she had escaped when she left this building?

Going around and behind the pond, there

was a shortcut to the Quad. Hesitating only a second, she took it. She could run if she needed to.

She had walked only a couple of hundred feet when she heard footsteps behind her. The sky was fully dark now, and the path had only one light at the beginning and another at the end. She glanced back and quickened her pace.

The footsteps quickened.

"Who's there?" She spun around to face whoever it was, fully expecting Stan Hurley to step out of the darkness.

"Abby, is that you? I thought it was. I didn't mean to scare you. It's me, Martin Beecher. You probably shouldn't be on this path alone."

"Martin?" She gathered her wits. "Why are you out here alone?"

"I followed you. Saw you come out of the chem building. Don't you know it's Friday night?"

As attracted to him as she'd been in the library, she wasn't sure now. Following her seemed a strange thing to do. She decided to take a light approach.

"Sure I know what day it is. I was just hurrying back to my room to change clothes. Some of us are going to the Tower. We're going to look through the telescopes for the monster."

He laughed. "Mind if I come along? If I saw

it, maybe I could believe in it. Last year a rumor got started that there was a ghost haunting this pond. A lot of people claimed to have seen it. Turned out it was a barn owl. A couple of bird-watchers ID-ed it. They thought it might have been living in the attic of the gym. When the gym burned down it moved here."

Her mind leaped from showing up with Stan Hurley to showing up at the Tower with Martin Beecher. A little devil whispered that it would pay David back for flirting with Sissy.

"Sure, join us. If you don't mind waiting a minute for me to change. When I was cleaning up, I spilled that awful soup the Quad Caf was serving tonight — the soup no one ate — all down my shirt. I'm tired of smelling like split peas."

Martin laughed. "No problem." He stepped up beside Abby on the path, and she decided she was glad for the company.

The building everyone called the Tower was really the Wesley Worthington Memorial Tower, built in memory of some ancient founder of Salem University. It was tall and narrow, twenty stories high. One room at the top of the structure housed a carillon, which was often played on Sunday mornings and for special occasions.

On the eighteenth floor were the offices for the campus radio station, WKSM. Other floors had more offices, a barbershop, bookshop, candy shop that made chocolate to die for, and a dry cleaners.

Several floors, including the top, had observation decks equipped with telescopes. Astronomy students used them, but so did anyone else who wanted a great view of the campus or a closer look at the stars. Last semester a student had been badly injured falling from one of the decks. Abby shuddered at the idea.

"They said they'd be on top." Abby punched the buttons for the twentieth floor. "And, Martin," Abby continued as the elevator closed and slid up quickly. "I'm sort of going steady with David Waters. You should know that."

"Sort of? That gives me a little hope, doesn't it?" Martin's blue eyes teased. "And I knew that. I see you around."

"You mean you've been watching me?"

"I mean I can't take my eyes off you. Does that feed your ego?"

"Does it ever. Thanks. But you might like Sissy King, too. She's a knockout. An actress, and really vivacious."

Martin laughed. "Don't worry. I'll behave. You don't have to set me up with someone else."

Jerry's loud voice made Abby's friends easy to find. Jerry was telling the plot of an old Abbot and Costello movie in which they meet Wolfman. She and Martin walked up and Jerry paused.

"Hi, guys. This is Martin Beecher. I ran into him wandering the campus alone and asked him to join us." Abby introduced her friends in turn. Only David acted as if Martin weren't welcome.

"Have you found the beast?" Martin asked.

"Not a growl or a fuzzy shape on the campus tonight," Jerry said. "We've found three couples making out in the bushes, a bunch of girls wading in the fountain, and the Omegas toilet papering Sigma Chi cars. Want to see? So far, they've wrapped four totally in paper. It's great." Jerry offered his telescope.

Sissy, as Abby could have predicted, took Martin's arm and led him to her telescope. David pulled Abby around the corner and into a dark recess of the balcony. Abby pressed her shoulders back into the building. She was afraid of heights. And startled by David's roughness.

"Where'd you pick up that guy, Abby?"

"I didn't pick him up. I ran into him the other night in the library. Literally. He picked up my books and we got talking. I think he's lonely. Sissy will take care of that."

"Just so you don't have to."

"Why, David, do I see you turning into a little green monster?" Abby put her arms around David's waist and looked up at him. There was just enough light to see his frowning face.

"Do I need to be jealous?"

"I don't know. If you have that need, I guess you can express it." She wasn't going to reassure him too much.

"I've been afraid you'd meet someone you liked better than me ever since we came here, Abby. I don't think you realize how attractive you are." David smoothed the out-of-control curls of hair away from her eyes. Ran his fingers down her cheeks. His touch sent shivers all through her body.

"Or how much of a grind? I'm sorry I'm so busy, David. Or so dumb I have to put in extra time studying. I hope you understand."

"I understand that I love you. And that I don't want to lose you. I'd do anything to keep from losing you."

Anything? She wondered what he meant by that.

He kissed her, but she held something back. His words should have made her feel wonderful. Why didn't they? Why did they make her feel a bit smothered? Trapped? Maybe she and David should date other people.

Am I crazy? Abby wondered. One minute I'm jealous of David, of Sissy flirting with him and him flirting back.

But when he said he'd do anything to keep from losing her, she felt just an inkling of fear.

Chapter 5

Jerry couldn't convince anyone to go to Vinnie's with him, so after everyone else returned to their rooms, he went alone. He was starving, and he knew he couldn't get to sleep without eating.

On his way home afterward, cutting through the woods near Nightingale Hall, the off-campus residence everyone called Nightmare Hall, seemed like a shortcut. The place looked really creepy at night, though, sitting there on that hill, tilted slightly to one side. One light burned on the porch, revealing a broken shutter on the front window. And one light was on in the attic. Did someone have a room up there?

Without meaning to, Jerry wondered what it would be like to die by hanging yourself — which was what a girl named Giselle McKendrick had supposedly done there. He also wondered what would make a person desperate enough to do such a thing. He was glad his parents had the money for a real dorm room. People still lived in the house since it was cheaper than the campus housing. He'd hate to live there. As much as he loved scary movies, watching them was one thing, living in one was another.

To tell the truth, he was a ninety-pound weakling, and he didn't care who knew it. Well, he weighed a hundred and twenty, but being only five foot four gave him an image he'd stopped trying to live down. After all, Dustin Hoffman was short. So were Michael J. Fox and Alan Ladd. He'd read that Alan Ladd had to stand on a box to kiss his leading lady. "Come back, Shane, come back," he whispered and smiled. As old as it was, Shane had been his favorite movie when he was a kid. His dad had a videotape of it, and Jerry had watched it over and over.

Although he'd never tell anyone, he missed his dad. They were both movie buffs. His dad liked scary flicks, too, and the old fifties science fiction films. Them. It Came From Outer Space. Forbidden Planet. He entertained himself by naming his favorites as he hurried through the woods. It was darker in here than he'd thought it would be.

A shuffling noise came from behind him. A

stab of fear clutched his middle. He glanced back, but saw nothing. Then it moved up beside him, and he could hear heavy breathing, panting actually, on his right.

He was just about to run when it leaped out in front of him. In the darkness he could make out only a giant blob, smelling of old socks and garlic, of rotten eggs and . . . and . . .

With a roar it attacked. He threw out both hands to stop it, but it was incredibly powerful. Remembering a movie he'd seen about a grizzly attack, he fell to the ground, scrunched up into a fetal position, covering his face and the back of his neck.

The thing stopped for a few seconds, studying him, he guessed. Then it took hold of Jerry's legs and began to drag him into the woods.

During the initial shock, Jerry had blocked all emotion. Now he started to shake. His insides turned over and being dragged did nothing to settle his stomach. Where was it taking him?

He wanted to cry but instead he shouted. "Let go of me! Get away, go away!" He tried to kick. For a second the beast lost its hold. He felt his foot connect with the big, hairy body. Twisting and turning, he tried to get up and run, but the beast grabbed him again, picked *him up, and flung him to the ground. The impact knocked the breath from his chest, and he gasped. I'll play dead, he thought. If it can't hear my heart pounding against my ribs.*

He would later think that the light had saved him, that first light of dawn. The beast seemed to raise up and look around. It snorted and groaned. Then slowly it shuffled away.

He lay still for what seemed like hours, but it was probably only five minutes. He wanted to be sure it was gone. It could be waiting for him to come back to life.

Finally, feeling that every inch of his body was bruised and bleeding, he got to his feet, looked around, and seeing nothing, made his way back to Devereaux Hall to get help.

As late as Abby came in, her roommate, Carrie Milholland, came in later. And as tired as Abby was — she had only slept a few hours at the most — she woke up when she heard Carrie crying.

"Carrie?" Abby sat up, feeling as if a truck had hit her. Oh, no, it was light. That meant she'd have to get up. She had an early shift at the cafeteria.

"Carrie, what's wrong? Are you sick?"

Abby's eyes focused enough to see the

bruise, red, but turning dark on Carrie's face and around her eye. "Did someone hit you? What happened?"

"Never mind, Abby. I'm sorry I woke you. I can't talk about it. I — I — It's too awful. I've done something awful. Leave me alone." She buried her face in her pillow and started to really bawl.

Abby moved over to sit on the bed beside her. She put her hand on Carrie's back and patted her as you would a crying child. She didn't know what else to do. Maybe Carrie had a fight with her boyfriend, but had he hit her? Or had she been raped? Maybe . . .

"You want me to call the resident advisor, Carrie? Maybe you need to report this. I could even call the police."

"No, don't! *Please* don't call anyone, Abby. I'll be fine. I promise you, I'll be okay. Go on to classes and leave me alone."

Abby sat there a few minutes longer, but she followed Carrie's wishes. She didn't call anyone. She took a shower and dressed. She'd go to work, then come home and go back to bed. There was no way she was going to function on so little sleep.

She was on her way out the door when the phone rang. She glanced at her bedside clock.

Who could it be so early on a weekend morning? She lifted the receiver. "Hello?"

"Abby?" It was David.

"David? What are you doing up? What's wrong?" She knew David so well that just hearing how he said her name told her something was wrong.

"Can you come over here right away? Jerry — Jerry's hurt. He says he's been attacked by a — the — the monster."

Chapter 6

This was a joke. It had to be a joke. But David had sounded upset, and concerned. He wasn't that good an actor. He could never pretend anything. He might be moody and possessive, but she always knew how he was feeling.

Abby scooted out the door without saying anything to Carrie. Carrie had her own problems.

There wasn't time to go down to the Quad Caf to say she was going to be late, or not get there at all. She hoped they had enough help to cover for her. She'd explain later.

Fortunately, no one was in the reception area to ask why she was running, or to stop her and ask what was wrong.

She covered the grassy stretch between the Quad and Devereaux in record time. David and Jerry lived on the second floor, room 213. She had teased them that it was an unlucky choice, but they had refused to buy into that idea.

David stood in the doorway waiting for her. She leaned into him and caught her breath. "This is a joke, isn't it, David?" she finally said. "Jerry is making this up from all that movie lore he has stored up."

"See what you think." David opened their door wider and she dashed to where Jerry lay on his bed. Gina sat beside him looking concerned.

Monster or not, Jerry had tangled with something. One shoe and sock were gone and his leg was all scratched up. His clothing was torn and disheveled and covered with dirt, leaves, and twigs. He was curled into a fetal position, face away from Abby, towards the wall.

"Jerry? Jerry, it's Abby. What happened?"

Abby and Gina took hold of him and tried to roll him over. He resisted, curling tighter. Abby began to think that maybe he wasn't pretending. This wasn't one of his many pranks. She looked at David, who shrugged and shook his head. He moved over and sat on the bed, too.

"Jerry. You're all right now. Turn over and talk to us. There's no one here but David, Abby, and me. Do you want me to call the police?" Gina asked.

Jerry groaned but rolled over. David had turned on the overhead light, since the day was gray and overcast and the room dim. Jerry squinted his eyes, trying to focus, but shut out the glare at the same time.

David stepped over and turned off the light. He snapped on the lamp beside Jerry's bed. "That better?"

Jerry nodded and tried to sit up. He moaned again and held his head.

"Get him something to drink," Abby suggested. "Something with sugar and caffeine. Do you have any Cokes or a Dr Pepper?"

Jerry and David had a small refrigerator in their room for late night snacks, but mostly drinks. David rummaged through it until he found a Dr Pepper.

"One left. His fav." He popped the top with a fizzing sound, then handed the cold can to Gina. She held it to Jerry's mouth until he'd sipped some and took the can himself.

"I'm sorry, Jerry," Abby apologized, thinking she could get him talking. "I was sure this was a prank you were playing on me, since I wouldn't listen to your horror stories earlier."

"This was horror all right. But it was real, Abby. This thing, this beast, is *real*. I saw it." Jerry was ready to talk.

"You didn't have too much pizza at Vinnie's?" David asked.

"Vinnie's? When did you go to Vinnie's?" Abby questioned.

"Last night. I was hungry. I'll never be hungry again." Jerry grimaced. "Except that I threw up my pizza after that thing left me for dead. I think it was the light. The dawn saved me. I think it can't stand the light."

"Jerry," Abby suggested. "Start at the beginning. Why weren't you with him, David? Why did you let him go to Vinnie's in the middle of the night all alone?"

David frowned. "I wasn't hungry. I wanted to go to bed. Besides, I may be his roommate, but I'm not his mother."

Why was David so defensive and grouchy? Abby wondered.

"There was still a crowd at Vinnie's," Jerry told them. "I joined them and ordered a pizza. By the time I got my order, it must have been, wow, it must have been two o'clock. Anyway, Vinnie wanted to close. We moved outside to finish eating. And talking. We got talking old movies and you know how — "

"We know, Jerry," Gina interrupted. "Get to the monster part."

"It was really late when I started home, but

I knew a shortcut back to the dorm. I gave Nightmare Hall a wide berth, but decided to cut through the woods. That's ironic, isn't it? I didn't want to meet the ghost of Giselle McKendrick, so I stumbled across the monster instead."

"This monster attacked you in the woods?" Abby was getting impatient.

"I heard it first, slobbering, huffing, and puffing." Jerry was starting to feel better and warmed to his story.

"That's the wolf in 'The Three Little Pigs,' Jerry." A part of Abby still didn't believe what Jerry was saying.

"I know you think I'm making this up, guys," Jerry said, his face serious. "But I'm not, really I'm not. The thing smelled rotten, like dirty socks and garlic and — "

"That's what Lenny said it smelled like," Abby added, remembering. "Swear, Jerry, swear on-on — " She looked around. "On your tattered first edition of Stephen King's *The Shining*. Swear you aren't making this up. That you really saw some creature out there."

Jerry placed his hand on the book. "I swear, Gina, Abby, David. I swear this thing attacked me. I was lucky it was so late. It started to get light, and I think it can't stand the light. It turned around and left. I could have been killed."

"You want me to call the police?" David asked, reaching for the phone.

"No. Listen, none of you wants to believe me, and you're my friends. You think the police are going to buy this story? If I hadn't lived through it, I'd never believe it myself."

"He's right," Gina said. "The police are going to laugh and say it's another hazing prank, just like Lenny's was."

"And I'm not even pledging a frat." Jerry sipped his drink. "Are there any chips left?" He pointed to a flattened Frito bag on the floor.

"You're hungry?" Gina sighed and reached for the bag. It was empty except for crumbs, but Jerry took it and dug inside.

"I told you I threw up when it left."

"If there's something dangerous out there, guys, we can't just forget this." Abby got serious. "We've got to do something. We need to warn the whole campus."

"I think we'd have to catch it before the cops would believe in it." Jerry looked at the scratches on his feet and legs. "I hope its nails aren't poisonous."

Abby shook her head. She was tired, so tired. "Why don't you shower, change clothes, and come eat breakfast, Jerry? I could still get in part of my work time."

"That's probably a good idea. If I hurry, will you guys wait for me?" Jerry swung his feet onto the floor and unbuttoned his shirt.

"Are you afraid to walk to the Quad Caf alone?" David teased.

"Of course not." Jerry kicked off his second shoe and stood up, wobbling a little.

Gina steadied him. "Maybe you should stay in bed, or shower and come back to bed. I could go get you a tray."

"No, no. I don't want to be alone. I'm not scared, just — just — well, try going through what I did and see how *you* feel. That thing was all covered with fur. I kicked it. I think I landed a pretty good blow. Let's go look for someone with a black eye or multiple bruises." Grabbing a towel from the back of a chair, Jerry padded down the hall to the shower.

He was back before Gina, Abby, and David could do much more than review what Jerry had told them and wonder about it.

He came into the room with his clothes wadded in his fist and the towel tucked around his waist. Abby turned her back as he went to get clean clothes. "Get a whiff of these," he said, tossing his pants and shirt from the night before towards David, Gina, and Abby.

Abby picked up Jerry's shirt and sniffed it. The cloth did have a foul, musty odor that wasn't body odor, no matter how much Jerry had sweated fighting off the beast. Dirty socks was a good description. Garlic, too, and a rotten, skunklike odor.

A shower, clean clothes, and the promise of coffee and Saturday's pancake menu loosened Jerry's tongue. He was almost back to his normal motor-mouth self, but without the zany joking manner. As they walked on either side of him toward the Quad, he started talking again.

"Several theories came to me while I was showering. If this thing is afraid of the light, it could be a werewolf, or a werebeast. They don't always have to be wolves. It could be something like Dracula. Dracula melts in the sun. His skin blisters and peels, and literally starts to melt."

Abby looked at David. David grinned and shrugged again. Neither knew what to think. Had Jerry staged this whole thing to get attention? Was he starved for notoriety?

"Of course, it could also be some supernatural monster. One frozen in the ice like the Thing. Now it's thawed out and confused and attacking out of fear of the unknown. Or it could be coming from inside someone. Like in *For-*

bidden Planet. The monster in that was coming from the *Id*. You know, someone's subconscious. That means it could be anyone on campus. It could be coming from inside you Abby, or David here. It prefers to attack someone it hates or has a quarrel with, but it can also attack at random."

They entered the Quad and walked down the stairs to the cafeteria with Jerry continuing to rattle on. Maybe it was aftershock. But Abby realized Jerry could talk all day about the different monsters he'd seen on film and television, the ones he'd read about in books and comics. Apparently he'd made a life study of monsters.

Wasn't it ironic that he had now been attacked by one?

Or *said* he had . . .

Chapter 7

Abby's strange day continued after lunch. She had gone back to her room after breakfast feeling completely dragged out. Carrie had pulled the draperies so that light in the room was dim. She was asleep. To study — to stay awake for any reason — would have taken more discipline than Abby had that morning, so, setting the alarm clock for eleven-thirty, she gave in to her fatigue and climbed into bed. Oh, heaven. She melted into her pillow.

She made it to lunch but the hour flew by in a blur with her making and handing out subs as fast as she could pile up slices of ham and cheese. Twice she dropped a sandwich handing it to her friend and coworker, Jessica Vogt.

"Wake up, Abby. You stay out all night?" Jess was half scolding, half teasing. "Didn't I warn you about too much partying?"

"To tell the truth, Jess, it was morning that

got to me. Have you heard anything else about this monster that's supposed to be loose on campus?"

"You don't believe those stories, do you, Abby? Rumors are always zipping around school. You should hear the stories they tell about Nightmare Hall. I live there, I should know. But this has to be one of the more bizarre stories I've heard."

"Jess, one of my friends says he was attacked last night."

"Do you believe him?"

"Sort of. He's a joker, but he really seemed shook up by the experience. And he did have scratches on his legs and bruises all over. He said this thing dragged him across the woods."

Jess piled lettuce and tomatoes on several sandwiches before she spoke. "Well, I do know this. Ever since Giselle McKendrick's death there've been plenty of strange things happening here at Salem."

Abby concentrated on slicing buns, piling on ham and cheese until she felt someone staring at her. Looking up, she found she was face to face with Stan Hurley. He grinned but said nothing. It seemed as if he were satisfied that he'd got her attention.

"Abby — "

"Huh?"

"Hand me the sandwich, Abby," Jess said. "You know you just can't let yourself get this tired. You'll get sick."

Abby tried to concentrate on what she was doing. Sometimes she thought Jess misunderstood that "friend" did not mean "mother."

"You want to talk?" Jess invited as they finished with the line of hungry students and got their own lunches.

"I — not right now, Jess, thanks. I'm not usually this sleepy. Don't worry about me."

Abby had seen Lenny Latham come through the line near the end of her shift. She grabbed a ham and cheese sub, a Coke, and a bag of potato chips, piled them on a tray, and headed for where he sat.

"Can I talk to you, Lenny?" She stood at the table where he ate alone. She didn't think his face looked bad. Just a few scratches like a cat might make. "Anyone sitting here?"

"Oh, sure." Lenny's face flushed red. He hurried to hide the book he was reading.

"Is that X-rated?" Abby teased. The book was a large, flat volume, but she hadn't seen the title.

Lenny nearly choked. He grabbed his glass of iced tea and drank half of it down. "No, no. I — I — " He pulled out the book. "Well, everyone is teasing me so much, I didn't want

— well — " With a sheepish grin he handed Abby the book.

The volume was called *Night Creatures*. Abby took it from Lenny and flipped through the pages. There were some really scary pictures, vampires and werebeasts and one called the Child-eater of the Black Forest, which was really the story of Hansel and Gretel. So much for nice little fairy tales. Against her will, Abby was sucked in. She paged through much of the book as she nibbled her potato chips.

"This is pretty gory stuff, Lenny," Abby said, handing it back. "Sounds like you think the monster that attacked you was real."

"Are you going to laugh at me, too?" Lenny was on the defensive.

"No, I'm not. I just wanted to hear your story myself."

"It wasn't a fraternity prank." Lenny relaxed.

"What makes you think that? Everyone else thinks it was. And you are pledging Sigma Chi, aren't you?"

"I was. I dropped out. That thing wasn't one of them, Abby. They aren't that good. The thing I saw — well, I don't think it was someone dressed up." Lenny told Abby the whole story.

In exchange, she told him Jerry's story. "A

friend of mine says he was attacked last night."

When she'd finished, Lenny said, "Do you think we should call the police? No one believed me, so we didn't call them after my experience. I felt foolish enough."

"We don't have any kind of evidence, Lenny. I can see why they'd think this thing was just a prank by upperclassmen. If we had some evidence, they'd have to believe us." Abby chewed on the hard roll and thought about what the police might do if they did believe Lenny's or Jerry's story. "Did you go back and search the grounds of the gym the next morning after you were attacked?"

"No way, man. You couldn't get me back there if — "

"If you were in a crowd? Would you show us where it happened if you had a lot of backup? Let's go look, Lenny. You'd like for people to stop laughing at you, wouldn't you?"

"I guess so. But I'm used to it." Lenny stared at his half-eaten lunch.

Abby's heart went out to him. She had no idea what it would be like to have everyone think you were a nothing person, but Lenny was giving her a hint. Without thinking, she reached over and took Lenny's arm, squeezed it.

"You have strange taste in men, Abigail

McDonald," a voice behind her said. "What happened to your boyfriend?"

The voice belonged to Stan Hurley. How dare he keep pestering her? Before she could lash out with an angry response, though, he was gone.

"I'm sorry, Abby." Lenny hung his head.

"Shut up, Lenny. Don't apologize for that nerd's manners. It's not your fault that he's singled me out to annoy. Get some backbone." Now she needed to apologize. She had taken her anger at Stan out on Lenny.

The funny result was that her harsh words worked. He grinned and sat up straighter. "Okay, Abby. I'll play monster-buster with your friends. What time?"

Abby hadn't consulted her friends, but surely Jerry would want to investigate this mystery further. And whatever Jerry wanted Gina usually went along with.

"Five-thirty. Let's get there before dark so we can look around. We'll go to Vinnie's afterwards and talk. Deal?" She put out her hand to Lenny.

He blushed again but took it with a firm grip. "Deal."

She hurried her half-eaten meal back to the kitchen and helped clean up as fast as possible.

She needed to get back to her room and call everyone. Jerry, David, Gina. Sissy? Yes, they needed all the help they could get. Martin? Why not? He seemed to like Sissy. And Carrie. She'd invite Carrie. She didn't know what her problem was, but maybe looking for a monster would distract her.

Abby left the Quad Caf feeling happy, but as soon as she got upstairs to the reception area, her good mood was squelched quickly.

Her roommate, Carrie, sat on a couch crying. The resident advisor, Allison Bennett, sat beside her. And across, at a small table, taking notes, hunched two policemen.

"Oh, Abby, I've done something awful."

What had Carrie done that made the police want to talk to her? Another memory hit Abby. Carrie's face was bruised.

"I kicked it, I kicked the monster. It should have bruises."

Could Carrie be the one scaring, attacking students? Why would she do that? But she was so tiny, so helpless-looking.

A line from the book Lenny was reading had stuck in Abby's mind. When an ordinary person shifts into a beast, he or she can have abnormal strength.

Many mornings Abby had waked to see that

Carrie's bed had not been slept in. Other nights she came in very late, tiptoeing so as not to wake anyone, but Abby was a very light sleeper. She always heard Carrie.

Was this possible? Was Abby living with the campus monster?

Chapter 8

There was no opportunity for Abby to ask her roommate about talking with the police. Carrie didn't show up before Abby left to meet her friends at the site of the burned-out Peabody Gym.

She had contacted everyone by phone and no one turned her down. It sounded like a fun thing to do on a slow Saturday night. Abby wasn't planning the meeting for fun, but she guessed it would be all right if they enjoyed their investigation.

On the walk over, Abby told David, Jerry, and Gina about seeing Carrie in the Quad talking to the police.

"You think she was confessing to being the monster?" Jerry asked. "No way. That thing that attacked me was big. Huge. Carrie Milholland is tiny."

"It was dark, Jerry," Abby argued. "And

you were being dragged. How could you see how big the thing was?"

"Well, I just know it wasn't Carrie Milholland."

"You mean you don't want to admit that Carrie could manhandle you." Gina punched Jerry and ran ahead, laughing. Jerry took off after her.

"He seems to have recovered nicely from his experience," Abby observed.

"If you want to know the truth, Abby," David said, "I think now that he's survived, he's enjoying it."

If she hadn't heard Lenny's story, she would have gone back to thinking Jerry was making this all up. But Abby realized the two incidents were very much alike — the sounds, smells, and the description of the thing.

Lenny was waiting at the gym for them. "Wow, thank goodness you showed up. I didn't like waiting here alone. It brought back that whole awful night. I was starting to hear things and smell things and — well, you're here now."

Abby made sure that Lenny knew everyone. Sissy and Martin finally showed up. Holding hands. Abby felt a twinge of jealousy.

"What are we looking for?" Sissy asked. "Martin and I'll search behind the west walls."

Sissy had chosen the darkest part of the ruin.

Darkness was closing in fast. The blackened hulk of the old building stood in silhouette against the lavender horizon. Cicadas started buzzing in the nearby woods. Otherwise an eerie stillness blanketed the ruin.

"You think it's still haunted?" Gina asked.

"Of course," Jerry answered. "Ghosts probably love this skeleton even better than the building itself."

"Look for anything that doesn't belong here," Abby said, cutting off talk of ghosts. "You said it had fur. Look for fur caught on bushes, footprints, anything suspicious. Let's break into twos and threes, but don't anyone go off alone."

"Are you kidding?" Sissy laughed and grabbed Martin's hand. They headed to the far side of the charred building.

Everyone had brought a flashlight. Soon the area looked like an army of fireflies with lights flickering on and off, in and out of shadows and behind the burned walls.

A scorched smell still floated in the air, probably from the recent rains. Abby took David's arm so they wouldn't get separated.

"Scared?" he teased.

"Of course." She snuggled close to him. But

as good as he felt, as warm, as much as she wanted to stop and hug him, she kept her eyes on the ground and bushes.

Her attention paid off. "Here, look here." She shined the light onto a bush with thorny branches. Reaching out, she pulled a tuft of hair from the limb. Just touching the stuff make her shiver. Here was some concrete evidence.

Taking a tissue from her pocket, she carefully wrapped the hairs in it and placed it back, deep in her jean jacket.

They had agreed that half an hour of searching was probably enough. Before they turned around, though, David pulled Abby close.

"I never see you alone anymore, Abby. Are you avoiding me?"

"Of course not, David."

"We used to go out without a crowd."

"I know. And I liked that. It's just that we all live together — sort of — so we end up running around together." Abby didn't think she needed to apologize. David knew that. He should know she wasn't avoiding him. "Let me go, David. You're hurting me."

He squeezed her arms tighter, and even in the dim light she could see the dark scowl on his face. "Not until you promise me we'll go out tomorrow night *alone*. To a movie. Or to

Hunan Manor for a Chinese dinner. It's usually quiet there."

"Okay, David. I'd like that. Now let's get back." The way David was acting was a little scary. She had never seen this side of him before. "You don't have any reason to be jealous."

"You sure?"

"Of course I'm sure. Do you see me going out every night with someone else? I'm either working or studying or — well, now, we have this to worry about."

"We don't have to worry about Jerry's monster."

For a minute it wasn't *Jerry's* monster she was worried about. She was seeing a bit of a monster in the guy she'd been going with for four years.

"Yes, we do, David. Jerry's our friend." Abby pulled away and went to where they'd planned to meet.

Jerry had taken charge. "Okay guys, now we'll walk over to Vinnie's but we'll go by the woods where I was attacked last night. I don't think this thing will come out with all of us there, so let's stay together."

"Did anyone find anything?" Abby asked.

Sissy giggled. "We didn't, did we, Martin?"

In the reflected glow from their flashlights,

Martin's face appeared flushed. "No monsters," he said.

"Well, I did." Abby retrieved her prize.

"Oh, disgusting," Gina said. Everyone tried to see the bunch of coarse fur at the same time.

"I'll pass it around. But be careful with it. Keep it on the tissue instead of handling it a lot." Abby sniffed the hair before she let Jerry take it. "It does smell musty, like a damp basement."

"I pass," Lenny said, when the tissue got to him. "I don't have to see or smell that again." He had been quiet the whole evening, surely reliving the horrifying night when he was the first victim.

"Let me have it." David stretched out his hand. "I'll take it into the lab tomorrow and see if I can identify it."

"Can you do that?" Sissy asked.

"Of course. Every animal's hair is different. This may belong to a bunny rabbit." David grinned at Sissy.

"Pretty tall rabbit, David," Abby said. "Remember I pulled it off of the top limb of that bush." She hated to trust anyone with what she'd found, but if she couldn't trust David, who could she trust?

They enjoyed the walk across campus. Then they entered the woods behind Nightmare

Hall. The woods where Jerry said he was dragged and clawed.

"I think we should split into pairs and search," Sissy suggested. "We can cover a lot more ground."

Abby didn't like the idea. She suspected that Sissy wanted more time alone with Martin. But everyone agreed with Sissy.

"You come with us, Lenny," Jerry invited. "You and I know what to look for."

The woods seemed bigger, darker, denser at night. Jerry must have been really tired to take this shortcut by himself. Most of the trees had leafed out, but a few still stretched bare, skeleton fingers toward the sky.

Abby entered the woods to circle counterclockwise, thinking David was behind her. She heard footsteps for a short time. Then she realized she no longer heard anything. Swinging around, she found she was alone.

"David?" She listened. "David, where are you?" Why was she whispering? "David!" she called louder.

No one. No sound except the echo of her own voice.

There. To the left. She strained her ears. It seemed as if she heard voices. Without looking down, she set off in that direction.

Wet moss covered the makeshift path she

followed. Before she could put her left foot down, her right skidded. She fell, hard. Sharp pain pierced her ankle as she landed on it.

"Oh, no." She tried to get up but her hands landed on the same wet, spongy ground, and slipped away from her.

For a couple of seconds she sat there, angry and feeling sorry for herself. Where was David? Why had he left her alone? If she couldn't hear anyone, then no one could hear her.

"David!" She yelled as loud as she could. "Jerry! Gina? Someone. Anyone?"

Trying not to cry, she pulled herself to her feet, actually onto her right foot, gingerly trying the left. Maybe it wasn't hurt badly. She could hobble until she found someone. She had to run into someone sooner or later . . . didn't she?

But what if she ran into . . .

No. She couldn't think about that.

Abby limped, cried out, limped again. Her second attempt wasn't quite so painful. Her ankle was sprained, but not badly. She might walk it off.

Hobbling as best she could, holding on to trees and the tips of bushes, she got back to drier ground. But still she saw no lights, heard no voices.

Where was her flashlight? Suddenly she realized she didn't have it. Thinking only of being able to stand up, she'd limped away, leaving it where it had landed when she fell. She couldn't go back down there and look for it. Her only thought now was to get out of these dark, creepy woods.

Abby bit her lip and tried to think, but her heart was pounding and her breathing was ragged. She had to calm down.

David was probably looking for her. It wouldn't be long before he realized they'd been separated. He should already have realized it.

Unless . . . Unless. . . .

Maybe he'd gone back to the group to see if Abby was with them. But what if he thought she could take care of herself? That she *wanted* to be on her own?

"David?" She tried again, but she had trouble forcing her voice out around the lump swelling in her throat.

Then she heard the soft rustle of someone — or something — on the path behind her.

"David?" She swallowed — hard. "David, is that you?"

No one answered. David would call back as soon as he heard her. Wouldn't he?

What if it wasn't David . . .

Chapter 9

Just then someone stepped out of the darkness.

"Oh, Martin!" Abby said with relief. "I was so scared." She threw herself into Martin's arms and started crying hysterically. "I thought — I thought — "

"It's okay." He patted her back. "You're okay. We were worried. No one knew where you'd gone. Where's David? I thought you went off with David."

"I don't know. He was behind me and then he wasn't." Abby hiccuped, sniffed a few times, started to gain control. Taking a tissue from her pocket, she blew her nose. "Isn't David with all of you?" Worry crept into the corners of her mind, taking the place of anger. Maybe David hadn't left her on purpose.

"No, we came back together and decided we'd better look for both of you." Martin continued to hold her close. She liked the warmth, the strength of his arms.

"Abby, what are you doing?" David's flashlight beam caught the two of them. Martin released Abby and stepped back.

"David, I didn't know where you were. And then I fell and lost my flashlight and . . . I sprained my ankle. I don't know if I can walk. What happened to you?"

"I was right behind you."

"You weren't." Anger replaced Abby's fear. And the anger kept her from feeling guilty about David finding her in Martin's arms. Martin had come for her. David hadn't.

"Maybe we'd better get back to the others," Martin said quietly. "Can you walk, Abby, or do you want us to carry you?"

"I can walk. But I may need some help."

David stepped forward and took Abby's arm. But his touch wasn't gentle like Martin's had been. He was obviously still angry.

Abby limped along, David supporting some of her weight. By the time they found their way into the clearing and beside the path where Jerry, Gina, Sissy, and Lenny waited, her ankle felt better. Not great, but better.

She shrugged off David's hand. "I'm okay now. I don't need help."

"Abby," Gina said. "Where were you? We thought the monster had dragged you off to his den."

"Yeah," Sissy agreed. "You scared us."

"I scared myself," Abby admitted. "I fell and lost my flashlight." She didn't say anything about David leaving her. Whether he did or not, on purpose, it felt that way.

"I think we all need something to eat," Martin suggested.

"Yeah, nothing wrong with us that a pizza won't cure." Jerry seconded the motion. "But we found some more monster hair, Abby. It proves I wasn't lying like you all thought I was."

"Jerry, we — " Abby started.

"Yes, you did. You thought I made up what happened last night. I swear I didn't. And neither did Lenny. Whatever it was, it was the same beast."

It wasn't that far to Vinnie's. Abby was determined to walk there on her own. And she did. Her ankle throbbed, but her stubborn refusal of help felt good.

She slid into a booth gratefully. David slid in beside her. Martin sat directly across, but she didn't dare look at him. She wasn't sure what she'd see registered on his face, but she didn't want to know what he was thinking.

Vinnie himself took their order. "Well, you all look like a barrel of fun. What's going on?"

"Have you heard about the monster on campus, Vinnie?" Lenny asked. "We've been looking for it."

"Sure. Didn't you see the sign?" Vinnie pointed to a big homemade tagboard poster over the counter, putrid green with red lettering.

MONSTER PIZZA. EVERYTHING ON IT. SLICED GUTS, SCRAMBLED BRAINS, EYEBALLS. THICKENED BLOOD.

"Oh, Vinnie, that's sick." Gina groaned and covered her face.

"Yep. But it's been my most popular item all week. Want one? Or two? Transfusions of Pepsi on the house tonight."

"Monster Pizza? Why not?" Jerry agreed. "I'm game. We'll start with two. And soon. We've been working hard."

"Un-huh." Vinnie scribbled on his order pad. "And I'm going to win the fifty-yard dash next weekend in the meet."

They laughed, but just for Vinnie. Abby suspected no one was in the mood for humor.

After they'd ordered, Jerry took charge of the conversation. "Okay, let's look at what we've got. Two eyewitness stories of this thing. Two tufts of hair."

"And a partridge in a pear tree." Sissy giggled, making Abby realize she had squeezed in on the other side of David. Why wasn't she sitting by Martin? Gina was sitting between Martin and Jerry. Lenny had pulled a chair to the end of the table.

Abby's eyes met Gina's expressive green ones. Gina raised her eyebrows but said nothing.

"Sorry," Sissy giggled again. "I couldn't resist that."

"Try to stay in control, Sissy." Jerry pretended to be stern. Anything but a grin on his face seemed false. "We don't have a very accurate picture of what this thing looks like, but — "

"Five fingers. It had five fingers," Lenny said. "Hey, *The Beast With Five Fingers*. Anyone seen that movie?"

"Peter Lorre." Jerry lit up. "He worked for a pianist."

"Yeah, after the pianist died, his disembodied hand came after everyone." Lenny leaned forward, setting his elbow down and wiggling his fingers. "Like in the Addams Family."

"The hand kept haunting them." Jerry and

Lenny were off. Abby looked at Gina again. She shrugged as if to say, there's no stopping them now.

"If nothing else comes of this night," Abby said quietly, "Jerry and Lenny have found each other."

"Kindred spirits." Martin smiled at Abby.

"Do I have to sit by them?" Sissy asked. "I changed my mind. Maybe the rest of us could even move to a different booth."

The two horror movie nuts ignored the remarks and took turns shouting out movie titles. *"The Beast Within." "Curse of the Living Dead." "Doctor Gore." "The Vampire Lovers." "I Was a Teenage Zombie."*

"You were?" Gina put a stop to it. "I'm not going out with you anymore, Jerry Todd."

"Jerry. Lenny. Will you two guys make a date for tomorrow night?" Abby suggested. "Let's get back to the subject at hand."

"And the food." Gina elbowed Jerry to remind him that the pizzas had been delivered to their table.

Abby felt better chewing on the crisp crust, juicy tomato sauce, and stringy cheese. She wrapped a long yellow thread of cheese over the end of her slice. "Here's something we need to think about. Let's say this beast is a real person by day, like the werebeasts in Lenny's book. What would cause a person to change to a monster?"

"A magic potion," Sissy said.

"Anger," David spoke for the first time since they'd sat in the booth. Abby wondered if she should think about the subtext of his statement. Not now.

"The person is disturbed," Martin added.

"Yeah, weird," Gina put in. "Like Stan Hurley."

"He's mixing some kind of magic potion in chemistry class," Jerry said. "Have you smelled it?"

"Several times." Abby pretended to choke.

"I gag every time I see him, without smelling any potion." Sissy held her nose. "He's really gross."

Abby thought of dropping a bombshell on the group by saying that Stan had sort of asked her out. But she decided that, under the circumstances, with David already out of sorts, she'd better keep that secret. Anyway, they would tease her unmercifully.

"According to my book," Lenny said, sipping his drink, "a person can just be unlucky enough to be born under a full moon. Kinda like on the wrong side of the tracks. There's a story in here about a woman who marries a werebeast.

She locks him out of the house on every full moon night. He goes out and sucks all the blood he needs for the month, and the next morning knocks and she lets him back in."

"You mean like: 'Hi, honey, satisfied now?' " Gina asked.

"Oh, that story really sucks, Lenny." Everyone groaned. Jerry grabbed the book that Lenny had taken from a backpack at his feet. "Let me see the picture."

"There are some really awesome pictures in here." Lenny opened the volume for Jerry. "Let me show you my favorite."

"There they go again." Gina sighed. "We've lost them."

"What can we do?" Abby joked, feeling somewhat better in the normal setting of Vinnie's. "They're perfect for each other. I'm so glad I could bring them together."

" 'Matchmaker, matchmaker,' " Gina sang.

While they laughed, Abby looked at Martin again. His eyes smiled at her. Did she dare think about it? Maybe he was pretending to like Sissy. Or maybe Sissy assumed he did — all the guys did, didn't they? — and she'd been the one holding his hand, making the advances Abby had observed.

Abby sensed an atomic explosion building in David, pressed against her because of the crowded booth. They were going to have to have a serious talk soon.

Jealousy turned people into beasts easily. She didn't really think her boyfriend of four years was shape shifting into a beast that attacked unsuspecting college students, but jealousy was as strong an emotion as anger, maybe stronger.

Suddenly the pizza looked like the description on Vinnie's sign, and she felt sick to her stomach. The blood seemed to drain from her whole body as if she'd been a vampire's victim. The restaurant grew hot and stuffy. She had trouble taking in enough air to fill her lungs.

"Would — would you let me out, David?" She half stood. "I — I think I'm going to be sick."

Once out, half standing, half leaning on the table, red-hot needles shot through her ankle, but she hobbled to the bathroom despite her pain.

Chapter 10

Everyone was willing to call it a night by the time Abby got back to their table. Maybe they were worried about her. Maybe the evening had been tougher on all of them than they'd realized. But everyone admitted to being tired.

"Should we take the shuttle?" Martin asked Abby. "Or can you walk back?"

"I'll walk. I may be slow, but we'll talk. And no shortcuts through the woods. Promise?"

No one wanted to cut through the woods, so they took the long way back to the dorms. About a block from the Quad, Abby rummaged through her pockets.

"I've lost my key, Gina. Do you have yours?"

Gina started to dig in the pouch buckled around her waist. "I may not. I never worry about it if I'm with you. You're so reliable." She pulled out billfold, sunglasses, tissues, comb, lipstick. "I've got *everything* except dorm keys." Gina laughed.

"Never mind, Abby, Gina," Sissy said. "I have a great idea. Both of my roommates went home for the weekend. Come stay in Devereaux. We'll have a slumber party."

Abby hesitated. A slumber party with Sissy was pretty far down on her list of fun things to do. And she was exhausted. Walking home had finished her off.

Gina was more enthusiastic. "Great idea, Sissy. That'll be fun."

Sissy expanded her invitation. "Everyone come in for a while. It's not that late. I have two new CDs, plenty of drinks, and a popcorn popper. We'll party."

"No party, Sissy, please," Abby begged. "I really am beat."

"I have to study tomorrow," Martin said. "I hate falling asleep in the library."

"No studying for me." Jerry punched Lenny. "Lenny and I have a monster movie marathon planned. We're going to start about three o'clock and you're all invited. We'll order in."

Abby looked at David. They had a tentative date planned. He didn't seem to remember. "I have to study tomorrow, too," she said. "I'll see what time I get finished, Jerry. But I don't know how you can take this so casually. Something really strange is going on and someone could get hurt — *badly*."

"Hey, we're serious. We're doing research. As soon as we review the categories for monsters, we'll know which category our monster belongs in. That should help us catch him."

"Yeah," Lenny added. "There are rules for monsters, just like there are for vampires."

"What if our monster doesn't know that?" Sissy said. "Is there a union for monsters? He'll be ostracized if he doesn't follow regulation monster behavior?"

The more they thought about a monster union, the funnier the idea got. At least it put them in a better mood.

"Monster rules. I'm so sure," Gina said as the girls reached Sissy's suite. "You have something we can sleep in, Sissy?"

Sissy pointed to a chest with lingerie hanging out of every drawer. "Next to the bottom. Help yourself."

Abby sat on one bed and watched as Gina pulled out wisps of chiffon. She usually slept in an oversized T-shirt. Her eyes met Gina's and they hid smiles from Sissy, who was rummaging in her closet.

"I think I have three clean towels." She tossed two on Abby's bed. "I don't know about you, but I need a hot shower. Let's do that and then we can talk." Sissy disappeared with an armload of soaps and shampoos, towels, and a silky nightgown.

"I'm not going to be much fun, Gina," Abby said, leaning back on the single bed opposite Sissy's. "I don't even think I can wobble into the shower."

"You might want to soak your ankle. I have a feeling you were lying about how it feels."

"Some. But even that is too much work. Toss me that silky turquoise thing. I'll pretend I'm Madonna and have a personal trainer coming tomorrow to give me a massage."

"Jane Fonda probably has a massage every day, too. Such luxury. Some day." Gina sighed and disappeared into the bathroom.

The third drawer of Sissy's clothes intrigued Abby. With no one there to see her, she gave in to her impulse to snoop. Hanging out was a sequined-dotted length of sheer material.

Abby pulled the drawer all the way out. This was obviously where Sissy kept her drama supplies. There were cans of grease paint in several colors, a witch mask, face putty, a booklet on the art of makeup. Abby flipped through that. Scars, witch noses, warts, disfigured chins and cheeks and foreheads.

The idea hadn't occurred to her before, but someone from the drama department could be dressing up to look like a monster. Someone with access to all the makeup and costumes kept there. Why would Sissy want to do something like hide and attack people? Anger, rage, jealousy — Abby ran through the reasons they'd listed earlier in the evening for someone turning into or pretending to be a monster.

Jealousy seemed the only one that suited Sissy. Jealous of whom? Jerry and Lenny had been the only ones attacked so far. Sissy had no reason for jealousy there. Unless they were just red herrings for the real attack, for injuring the person she really wanted to get at. And who would that be? Abby shivered. Sissy might be jealous of her. Of David loving her. But enough for an elaborate scheme like dressing up as a monster and scaring people until she hurt the one she wanted?

No, that was crazy, Abby decided.

Putting things back, trying to remember which piece of material was hanging out — as if Sissy would remember herself with this cluttered room—Abby spotted a piece of paper folded small on the bottom of the drawer. She picked it up.

Curiosity drove her. Quickly she unfolded it. Her heart skipped a beat. She would know David's handwriting anywhere, his spidery scrawl.

Sissy, Sunday won't work. I'll meet you Tuesday night at ten at Varsity Pond, the west side where there are benches.

Wanting to wad the narrow rectangle, Abby folded it quickly and tossed it back in the drawer. Then she slid it almost shut, tugged off her pants and shoes, preferring to sleep in the shirt she was wearing instead of one of Sissy's nightgowns. She pulled covers up over her, turned her face away from Sissy's bed, and pretended to be already asleep.

They didn't know it, but Sissy and David were going to have company for their secret date — meeting — assignation . . . Abby didn't like this at all.

Swallowing over and over as her throat swelled, she squeezed her eyes shut and tried not to sob as she heard Sissy and Gina whispering and giggling.

You won't be laughing on Tuesday, Sissy, when I catch you with my boyfriend.

Anger flashed over Abby. She clenched her fists and silently beat her pillow. Anger was easier to live with than jealousy. But it was going to be a long time before she could sleep.

Chapter 11

The hours before ten o'clock Tuesday night seemed to number into the hundreds. They weighed on Abby like a ton of bricks instead of minutes and seconds.

She went to classes, studied, tried to study. Both Monday and Tuesday nights she went to the chem lab and worked on her extra-credit project.

Tuesday night Stan was in the chem lab before her, since she'd spent time in the library before going there.

He was no longer the least bit friendly, ignoring Abby while she got settled. Thank goodness her table was clear across the room from him. But then she could feel daggers of anger and hatred coming across the room into her back. Geez, she had just refused to go out with him. Was that such a crime? And he knew she was going out with David, so he shouldn't have been surprised at her saying no.

The rotten egg smell from whatever he was stirring and heating floated across the room and mixed with the equally acrid smell from her experiment. Two mad scientists competing for worst mess of the year. That's what hers looked like — a mess. She couldn't see his mixture, but if the appearance matched the smell, it was probably gooey, green, and black, with just a touch of khaki brown.

Suddenly, before she was ready, it was quarter to ten. She had to stop if she was going to get to the pond at the same time as David and Sissy. She covered her mixture and placed it in one of the class freezers.

She turned to go and was surprised. When had Stan left? She must have really been concentrating if she hadn't heard him. But then he had the ability to creep around like a hyena hunting.

Outside, a light spring drizzle had stopped and fog had formed. Thick fog. She could scarcely see ten feet ahead of her. The trees across from Griswold Hall loomed suddenly as she crossed the grass and neared the pond.

Keeping off the sidewalk, she walked in complete silence around the south end of the water. Twice she thought she heard someone behind her, just a slight scuffling in the grass, once a crunch of gravel, a whisper of weeds crushed.

She glanced around, but of course could see nothing in the thick, gray, cottony air. She might have arrived before David or Sissy. She needed to be careful not to stumble across either of them. That would certainly spoil her plan to hide and listen.

She needn't have worried. Because what she spotted near the benches, just where they said they'd meet, was two bodies twined into one. Sissy and David. Kissing.

Abby bit her lip, holding back sudden tears and a sob. She should have been angry. All she felt was a huge ball of sadness pressing on her chest, her heart.

What should she do? Scream and rage at David and Sissy? Let them know she had seen them? Slip away, sneak into the bushes like a whipped dog? Pretend she didn't know, and wait for David to confess? For him to say, what we had is over, Abby. I want to go out with Sissy. We're tired of hiding.

She felt dizzy with confusion, disappointment. But then a muffled sound behind her snapped her back to the fact that she was alone in the woods with some beast on the loose.

She smelled the garlicky mustiness of the body, the furry body. It mingled with the wet fog to clog her nostrils and smother her. She swung around, fell to the ground as it roared and stomped.

Dimly, through the haze she had dropped into, she heard Sissy scream. David yell. She heard the scuffle, the fighting, the scrambling to try to escape.

When she came to, she realized she had fainted. Where were David and Sissy? Were they hurt? She got to her feet, bent double with a wave of nausea, breathed, breathed, stood straight again. She moved forward in slow motion, swimming through the suffocating fog, fighting to surface from it.

She found the park benches. Glanced around. Here! Here was a tuft of hair, some clumps of fur. What had happened to David and Sissy? Had the — monster — carried them off? She started to call out, then remembered they hadn't known she was there. If she revealed herself, they'd know she was watching, spying on them. Did it matter now? One of them, both of them, might be lying someplace near here, badly hurt.

She searched but found no body, no bleeding Sissy on the ground. No David leaning over her. Or the opposite. Oh, please, don't let David be hurt. She forgot the hurt he had caused her, the heartache.

Smells lingered on the air. But all sound was again muffled in the thick clouds surrounding her.

Quickly she made her way back to the sidewalk in front of the chem building. A small crowd had gathered.

She ran.

"David?" She recognized him standing just outside the circle around Sissy, pretending he wasn't with her. Blood oozed from one long scratch on his face. "David, what happened? I — I was going home from working late in the lab when I heard this terrible noise. Sissy? Are you hurt, Sissy?"

Sissy was crying but she didn't appear to be badly hurt. In fact, she appeared to be enjoying the audience around her.

"I — I was coming home from rehearsals — you know I got the lead in the spring play — "

"We know, Sissy. We know," muttered Abby to herself.

"Well, I was walking along, in a hurry to get home, but not walking too fast because I couldn't see, when this thing jumped out at me. I knew what it was immediately and I screamed and screamed. That was probably what saved me. It got scared and ran, ran into those woods, there. We probably should see if we can find it, but with this fog — Well, I was just lucky. I have a few scratches, but I'm really not hurt. Just scared. God, I was scared." Sissy leaned on Gus McClain, a hefty handsome linebacker for the Salem football team. He grinned, glad to hold her up if she felt faint.

"David Waters happened to come along," Sissy continued her drama. "He stopped and fought the thing off. He's not hurt badly, but he may have saved my life."

Abby's eyes met David's. Something passed between them. A realization, maybe not that Abby had seen David and Sissy together, but a realization that Sissy was lying. And a realization that something they had treasured for four years was gone. They still needed to talk. He had "forgotten" their date for Sunday night. But a discussion would be merely a formality. Abby saying, here's your tennis sweater back. I hope it won't be too, too big for Sissy. David might even say, I didn't mean to hurt you, Abby. It just happened.

She spun around and walked smack into Stan Hurley.

"Can I walk you to the Quad, Abby? It's not safe for you to be out here alone. I'm going that way anyway."

Something told Abby that Stan had seen Sissy and David together. That he knew she and David were no longer going steady. But if he thought —

No, right now he was just being nice. Nice didn't fit the image they had all formed of him, but that was all right.

She fingered the small fluffs of hair in her pocket. A scenario formed in her mind. Stan had waited outside Griswold Hall for her to come out. He'd followed her to the woods. He, too, had seen David and Sissy kissing.

Had Stan known that Abby was hurt by what she saw? Had his anger at someone hurting her made him shift to the beast and attack the couple? He had done this for her? Questions, too many questions buzzed around her head, making her feel dizzy again.

Why was she such a wimp? If she hadn't passed out, she would have seen this thing. Would she have known it was Stan?

Jumbled thoughts whizzed through her mind. She felt more confused than ever. And she was tired.

"That would be nice, Stan. I'd like to go to my room."

She fell into step beside him. He didn't say a word the whole way to the Quad. But that didn't matter. She was safely back to her dorm. Left with a lot of heartache and as big a puzzle as ever.

But safe. For now.

Chapter 12

David shivered, thinking about what had happened to Sissy and how lucky she was to have gotten away from that — that thing that attacked them. Attacked her, actually. The beast had knocked him aside and jumped on Sissy, rolled her away from him into the dense fog.

For much too long he had frozen, his legs locked, his heart pounding, unable to react. He knew the sounds were going to haunt him forever, the moaning, the growls, Sissy screaming.

How she had gotten away from it, he didn't know, but here she was now acting like a celebrity, talking to anyone who would listen, telling the tale over and over.

That was one of the things he didn't like about Sissy. Her need for attention. Her over-dramatizing everything that happened. Even her demands, her delight, it appeared, at their secret meetings. David had started wanting to tell Abby about Sissy right away, but Sissy demanded that they keep quiet, meet on the sly.

What he was doing ate away at his insides, making his stomach ache. Every time they were all together, he found himself stiff and unlike himself. He couldn't even talk and laugh and enjoy anything in a normal manner.

Now, tonight, looking at Abby, he felt worse than ever. She knew. He was certain that she knew. Why hadn't he taken her aside right then, while Sissy was holding court, and talked to her? Confessed everything? There was no way to keep from hurting her. At least he could make a clean wound so they could both start to heal.

Abby might not believe that this was hurting him, too. But he had dated her for four years. He had loved her. He still loved her, but something inside him had started to feel trapped. And maybe, if he wanted to admit it, curious. Curious about other girls. How it would feel to kiss someone else, hold someone else in his arms.

He settled onto one of the park benches near the pond, deep in thought, not realizing he might still be in danger. Sissy was never going to miss him. She had her audience to think about.

The musty smell sent him into immediate panic.

He swung around, peering into the fog. Because of the clouds swirling and shifting around him, he couldn't tell where the sound of shuffling feet was coming from.

But it was coming, coming for him.

Suddenly the monster leaped out of the gray void and grabbed him.

Falling to the ground, David grasped it and rolled. The hairy arms were strong as steel bands wrapping round his chest. A snarl from its snout carried a fetid breath. The stench of a decaying carcass, the heat of anger and evil.

Sharp claws raked his face. He threw his hands up to protect himself and felt razorlike teeth rip his skin.

He was able to throw it off and struggle to get to his feet only to be tackled from behind. The creature clawed his back. His jacket shredded like paper. He felt it rake his back, then squeeze. He choked, his breath wheezing out like air from a broken balloon.

Lashing back and forth, he gasped for air but felt the coppery taste of blood fill his mouth instead.

David's last thoughts before he lost consciousness were of Abby. How he had wronged her. How he was going to die before he could apologize to her.

His mind returned to all the good times they'd shared . . . the dinners . . . the long walks . . . the picnics —

Chapter 13

The woods. They were in the woods. Abby and David. They had brought a picnic. Abby had fried chicken, made potato salad, and sliced the chocolate cake her mother had made the day before, piling up generous pieces, since she knew David would like it.

After lunch they dived into the deep pool from the big rocks around the creek where it had dammed up years ago and formed this perfect swimming hole. Then they lay in the sun on side-by-side towels, holding hands until they were scorching, needing another dip.

"Look, Abby. Wait till you see this — look!" David poised, leaning backwards off the highest rock.

"Don't, David. Don't jump. You could hit your head," Abby cautioned, her hand stretched out to him.

"No, I won't. You worry too much!"

He leaped up, arched, then headed for the water. He was too close to the rock, too close to the bottom rock.

"David, watch out!" Abby cried. She jumped up and reached for him but it was too late. He was going to crash into the rocks.

She stretched out her hand and reached and reached and reached . . .

Suddenly she sat straight up in bed and screamed. "David!"

He didn't hit the rock. She was dreaming. She was in her own bed, at Salem University. This was another year. She and David weren't swimming together. They might not even be going out anymore.

All that flashed through her head before she realized that something else had waked her.

"Something has happened to David," she whispered. "David is hurt!" She jumped out of bed, wide awake, and started to tug on her jeans and a sweatshirt.

Before she got her tennis shoes laced, there was a pounding on her door. She snapped on the light, no longer worried about waking Carrie. Then, as she dashed to her door to unlock it, she saw that Carrie wasn't in her bed.

She jerked the door open to find Jerry and Gina in the doorway. "Abby, you have to come with us," Jerry said urgently.

"What's wrong?" Abby looked from Jerry to Gina, standing beside him, her face contorted into a mask of worry and concern.

"It's David." Gina reached out and took Abby's arm. "It's David, Abby. He's hurt. Get your jacket. It's raining." Gina pushed Abby back into her room and towards her closet.

Her jacket wasn't in the closet. She must have tossed it someplace last night. That didn't matter now. She grabbed a rain slicker and a yellow, plastic-brimmed hat.

"What happened?" Abby asked. "How bad is he? He'll be all right, won't he?" She grabbed Jerry's arm and swung him around. "Tell me he'll be all right."

"They don't know," Jerry said. "And we haven't seen him yet. Sissy called me. She went looking for him, heard him moaning, and found him beside the lake. She said she didn't know why he'd gone back there. It was the same place the — the beast had attacked her earlier."

"Maybe he went back to look for clues." Gina took one of Abby's arms and Jerry took the other. They steered her towards the stairs, down, out the front door of the Quad, and then towards Gina's car.

"Where is he?" Abby asked, her legs feeling rubbery. She was glad for Jerry and Gina's arms. She wasn't sure she could walk without them holding her up.

"In the hospital." Gina took the wheel, started the car, backed and swung onto the street. "Sissy called Jerry from there. She needed someone with her."

Jerry leaned over the backseat, put his hand on Abby's shoulder, and squeezed it. "You know Sissy, Abby. She probably got hysterical and called an ambulance. They took David to the hospital as a precaution."

Abby's mind turned to stone, stone as hard as the rock David was going to crash into in her dream. By the time they reached the hospital and Jerry helped her from the car, she felt numb all over. They steered her into the emergency entrance and up to the desk.

The smell of antiseptic and fear surrounded her. A cart with a sheet-draped figure rattled past her, stern-faced nurses on either side, pushing. She grasped the cold counter as Jerry asked about David.

"We've come to see about David Waters," Jerry told the nurse at Admitting. "He was brought in tonight with — with — He came from the campus. I don't know what kind of wounds he had."

The nurse looked at her book. "He's in surgery. You can't see him. But you can wait if you like."

Did she think they were going to turn around and go home? Abby thought. Of course, they'd wait. But Jerry and Gina had to pry her hands off the counter and push her towards an orange plastic chair.

"I wonder where Sissy is?" Gina wondered, looking around.

As reality hit her, Abby wished she could have stayed frozen. Her hands started to shake and she felt as if she were going to throw up.

"I'll get us some Cokes, Abby." Jerry stood up, leaving Abby with Gina. "That'll settle your stomach."

"Abby, get hold of yourself," Gina ordered. "We don't know that David's hurt bad."

"He's in surgery."

"If that thing scratched him, he may have had to have stitches."

"They don't take you to surgery for stitches." Abby had gotten plenty of stitches in her life. She had been clumsy even as a child.

Two police officers followed Jerry back into the reception room.

"What did you do, Jerry?" Gina whispered. "Steal the Cokes?" She took the red can Jerry handed her.

Jerry looked around and grinned. "Hey, I paid for them," he told the officers. "You're following the wrong guy."

Leave it to Jerry to keep his sense of humor no matter what was happening, Abby thought.

The dark-skinned police officer smiled and took off his hat. "I'm ready to ask you to go steal me one, too, son. This has been a busy night. Two car wrecks — now this." He sat beside them, motioning his partner to pull up a chair. "I understand David Waters is your friend."

"Yes." Abby nodded. "Do you know anything about David? Is he all right? Will he be all right?"

"I can't answer that right now, but I'll try to find out for you," said Officer Mooney, who introduced himself and Officer Rodgers, his partner.

"What do you know about this — this — beast that Sissy King said attacked her tonight, and David later?"

Officer Rodgers filled in as much as he knew. "We think some crazed animal jumped David. He was all scratched up. His arm is broken, but he could have fallen on it when this thing jumped him."

"But Miss King called it a monster and said this wasn't the first time it had attacked someone." Mooney took out a notebook.

Abby looked at Jerry. "No one has been hurt badly before," she said. "We've thought it was a joke, a fraternity prank, or someone trying to scare us."

What did she mean, *trying*?

"Why hasn't anyone called us before?" Rodgers wanted to know.

"Officer," Jerry said, his face serious for a change. "What would you have done if someone had called and said there was a monster attacking people at Salem University? That a pledge for Sigma Chi was attacked while spending the night at the Peabody ruins for his hazing? That I was jumped while I was cutting through the woods at about four A.M. one night?"

Rodgers looked at Mooney, who grinned. "Well — " Mooney started to say.

"Exactly." Jerry stopped him. "You would never have believed us. This is the first time someone has really been hurt."

"And now you think it's an animal?" Abby reminded them.

Rodgers studied Gina, Jerry, and Abby.

"You three look to be eighteen or nineteen. Do you still believe in monsters under the bed?"

"The monster was in the woods," Gina said with a straight face. "Not under our beds or in our closets, Officer. We've told you all we know. Call it whatever you like, but it would seem like you should investigate it before it kills someone."

Mooney looked at Rodgers and the two of them stood up.

"I'll report to you as soon as we know your friend's condition," Mooney said.

"Thank you," Abby said. "That's kind of you. And can we see him?"

"That's not up to us." Officer Rodgers took off for the reception desk. Mooney touched his hat with the tips of his fingers, smiled at Abby, and followed his partner.

"The secret is out." Jerry leaned back and sipped his Coke.

Gina picked up an old copy of *People* magazine. A smiling Willard Scott stared at Abby from the TV screen in the corner. Gina flipped the pages without looking at them. "Surely they'll believe David's story."

No one said, if David can tell them. Abby wadded a tissue up in one fist and gripped the cold Coke can with the other.

About an hour passed with no news and no

sign of Sissy. If she had called Jerry wanting company, where was she now?

Gina curled up on an empty couch and dozed off. Jerry flipped through magazine after magazine. Abby couldn't seem to focus on anything. She watched the busy emergency room crew come and go and wondered about all the other lives unfolding around them. Anything to keep from focusing on her own. Or David's.

Her heart leaped though, when she spotted Officer Mooney, face grim, walking towards her.

Chapter 14

"I never heard a stranger story except in a grade B movie." Officer Mooney scratched his chin. "But the nurse says you can go in to see David, Abby, since all he's done is call your name. He's awake, but covered with about a million stitches. They don't want him to have any other visitors until he's feeling stronger."

"I guess we'll wait for you here, Abby," said Gina. "Wish we could go in with you." Gina gave Abby a sympathetic look. "Hug him for us."

"I will." Abby hurried off in the direction that the nurse pointed.

She reached the surgery waiting room just as she saw Sissy hurrying towards her. "Abby, have you heard anything? Can we go in to see David?" Sissy grabbed her arm.

How could she tell Sissy this? In plain language. "I can, Sissy. No one else yet. But I'll come right back and tell you what he says."

Sissy collapsed on a couch. "I'd appreciate that."

Abby stopped and took a deep breath when she first saw David. He looked like a mummy. His face was covered with bandages and his plaster-covered arm was bent in an L and hung in a sling. His eyes were closed.

Abby cautiously sat on the side of the bed and gently touched his good arm. "David? Are you awake?"

"Um-hum. Abby, is that you?" His brown eyes flashed open, and David struggled to sit up. "Oh, Abby, I'm so sorry. I thought I was going to die before I could say that. I know I've hurt you, and I didn't mean to. It just happened."

"It's all right, David. I know I haven't been much fun since we came to college. I'm just so uptight about making good grades and keeping my scholarship."

"Hush." He tried to smile, then grimaced. "I must look awful."

"Are you in pain?" Abby asked, changing the subject. She had a feeling David would no longer be beautiful. She felt sick when she thought about his beautiful skin, never a blemish, always so healthy looking.

"No, I had a shot. I thought that thing was going to kill me, Abby. And I — I was so scared."

"Anyone would be. You're going to be famous when you get out of here, though. Prepare for that. Sissy may have to fight off the sympathetic women."

"You talked to her?"

"Not about — about you two. She's outside. They won't let her in to see you. She said hi."

"You're a good sport, Abby." David's voice trailed off and his eyes closed. Abby could see that he was gone for the moment.

She stood, took a deep breath, and left him. Did she want that chiseled on her grave? Here lies a good sport. She guessed it was better than some other epitaphs.

But what was she doing thinking about dying?

By the time she talked to Sissy and got back to the waiting area, she felt totally exhausted. Her legs wobbled. Her whole body felt like a puppet's wooden frame when the puppeteer loosens the strings.

"I've got to go get some sleep, Gina. I don't even know if I can make it back to the Quad."

Gina supported Abby on one side, Jerry the other. "We're all tired, Abby. We can't do any more for David tonight. Let's go home and crash." They helped Abby into the car and drove back to campus.

Abby meant to go straight to sleep, but it was getting light when she opened the door to her room and headed for the inviting single bed.

Maybe it was the musty, rotten odor that stopped her.

It couldn't be in here, could it?

A whorl of fear ran up and down her spine. She glanced at the closed closet door. Leaning over, biting her lip, she looked under the bed.

Mother, there's a monster under my bed. Come quick.

Monsters in the closet, monsters under the bed, the boogie man will get you if you don't watch out.

Watch out. Watch out.

The words echoed through her aching head.

She swung around. And a strange sight caught her eye.

On Carrie's pillow, on her perfectly made bed, were tufts of hair. It looked as if there'd been a cat fight. She had a vision of yowling, shrieking, clawing sounds. A whirling, twisting ball of two cats spitting, spinning, both frantically out of control. She had watched her own tomcat, Dirty Harry, too often to keep the picture at bay.

But this was not cat hair. Cats were not gray-green and brown. Cats didn't smell like rotten eggs. They weren't allowed in the dorm. Freshmen couldn't have pets on campus.

No pet had left this fur behind.

Reaching out, Abby collected the evidence. The hair had the same coarseness as the tufts she'd found before — out by the pond.

Carrie, oh, Carrie. I didn't really suspect you before. Why would you do this?

And where are you now?

Chapter 15

As tired as she was, she knew she couldn't sleep now. She collapsed on her bed and slowly dialed the number on the card Officer Mooney had given her. The dispatcher transferred her quickly to Mooney's car. He promised to come right to the Quad.

She hurried to Gina's room. She didn't want to talk to the police alone. Pounding on Gina's door as softly as possible so she wouldn't wake the whole wing, she whispered loudly.

"Gina, are you asleep yet? I need your help."

Gina, in a robe, rubbing her eyes, clicked the lock, pulled her door open a crack. "Abby? I thought you were going straight to bed."

"So did I. But I found something that woke me up. Listen, Officer Mooney is coming over here and I wish you'd be with me when I talk to him."

Gina stopped yawning and her eyes widened.

"The police? Come in, Abby, quietly. My poor roommate thinks I never sleep. And wishes by now that I'd move out. I'll get dressed."

Gina pulled on the clothes she'd tossed on a chair by her bed. She pulled a brush through her short, pixy hair, then pushed Abby back out the door.

"What happened?" she asked as they hurried downstairs to let Officer Mooney into the dorm.

"I — I think I've found out who the monster is. I think it's Carrie."

"Carrie Milholland? Your roommate? She's barely five feet tall. How could she attack those guys?"

Officer Mooney and his partner were waiting in the lobby when Abby and Gina got downstairs.

Abby was so tired she felt a bit dizzy. But she knew this was important.

The two policemen followed the girls upstairs to Abby's room where Abby handed them the ball of fur.

"You found this on Carrie Milholland's bed?" Mooney asked. He smelled it and rolled it around between his fingers.

"Yes, when I came home from the hospital."

"Isn't this the same girl we talked to the other day?" Officer Rodgers asked Mooney.

"Yes, she has some . . . problems." Mooney

didn't say what they were. Abby knew he couldn't tell, but she wished she could ask.

"She's hardly ever here at night," Abby added. "And the other day she said she'd done something awful, but she didn't tell me what it was." She gave Office Mooney a chance to share if he knew.

"Hummmm." Mooney nodded. "Abby, did it occur to you that someone might have put this fur here? While you were at the hospital."

Abby's mind was fuzzy. She thought that over. "Someone is trying to scare me?"

"You don't really believe this is some kind of a monster, do you?" Rodgers grinned slightly.

"Well — " Abby looked at Gina who shrugged as if to say, what did you expect from the police? "You think it's someone dressing up like this and attacking people? Who would do that?"

"If we knew, then we'd talk to him. Arrest him. Think that over, Abby. Make a list of people you could suspect of doing something like this. Maybe it was a prank that got out of hand. But stop thinking it's something supernatural. That's for the comics and the movies." Mooney's grin was sympathetic, but Abby could see he thought her imagination had run away with her.

"And get some sleep," Mooney continued. "I'll take this fur to the lab and have them run some tests."

"We've found fur before," Gina thought to say. "One of the guys has it, I think. It was just like this."

Rodgers laughed outright. "The monster's costume must be getting threadbare by now." He followed Mooney down the hall.

"They think we're nuts, Abby. They were just being nice about not saying it." Gina sat on Carrie's bed. "You afraid to sleep here by yourself? I can sleep on Carrie's bed."

"Would you, Gina?" Abby said. "Maybe I could feel safe then."

"Yeah, I'll protect you." Gina laughed. She wasn't much bigger than Carrie. Abby always felt gigantic around her, even though she wasn't much over average height.

Before Abby dozed off, she said, "We'll find Carrie later, Gina. We'll follow her and find out where she's going at night."

The next morning Abby cut her nine o'clock class and hurried to the hospital. David was sipping orange juice through a straw, sitting up in bed. He must feel stronger, Abby realized.

She perched on the edge of the crisp white

bed sheets and squeezed his hand. "How long will you have to stay here?"

"They want to make sure no infection sets in. They think an animal attacked me, and animal claws have tons of germs. I might have to start rabies shots today."

"Did you *see* what attacked you, David? The police think your attacker might have been someone dressed like a monster."

"I couldn't see very well. It was dark and foggy, and I was busy trying to get away from it. If this is a person, he's sure strong."

There was a moment of silence between them. A moment where Abby could feel David's fear. His fingers traced her hand, then took a strong hold.

"I'm going to have a lot of scars, Abby."

"You'll still be handsome." Abby tried to be reassuring, but David looked doubtful. She wanted to stay with him, to cheer him up, because he seemed so shaken by the attack. But she couldn't miss her next class.

"I'll come back." She told David when she got up to go. "We all will. You can have other visitors this afternoon. I asked." She rushed out and down the hall, and caught the shuttle back to campus to get to Griswold by ten.

Jerry rushed over to her as she came into the classroom. "How's David?"

"Go see him this afternoon, Jerry. He needs your sense of humor. I think he's lost his. He's really down today."

Abby dumped her books at her table and hurried over to the lab half of the room. Stan Hurley stopped her.

"You went to the hospital? How's David?"

Abby stared at Stan. His hair stuck up wildly on one side as if he'd slept on it funny. She had a strange urge to touch those kinky curls. Would they be coarse? Abby hadn't crossed Stan off her list of suspects. It seemed much more like something he'd do. And she could see that he was strong enough.

"Do you really care, Stan?" Abby snapped. She whirled around and gripped the counter by her station. Pulling out the drawer with her name on it, she set out test tubes, rubber tubing, tongs. She didn't even know what the assignment was for today, but she needed to keep busy until Stan walked away.

She felt his eyes burn into her, but she kept her own averted.

The experiment was easy. She finished it in a few minutes, entering the results and her notes into her lab notebook. Then she took the rest of the period to mess with her extra-credit work.

When she finally looked around the room,

Stan had his back to her, engrossed in his own work. She breathed a little more smoothly, but she felt dead tired. She could lie down on the floor right now and sleep for days.

"Jerry, where's Gina?" She had finally realized Gina wasn't in class.

"She's got the stomach flu." Jerry moved over beside Abby. "Said to tell you the plans you made last night are out for her. To wait until tomorrow."

Abby looked at Jerry. "She really just slept in, didn't she? I know I wanted to."

"No, I stopped to get her, and she pushed past me and ran to the bathroom."

Our plans can't wait until tomorrow, thought Abby. I don't know how I'll find Carrie, but when I do, I'm going to keep an eye on her by myself.

Abby had to work in the Quad Caf for the dinner shift. She was glad, since she realized she missed David being with them. He didn't always talk a lot, but she was used to his being around. Jerry waved at her as he entered the cafeteria, then took a seat next to Lenny. Every time she looked at them they were waving their arms and talking nonstop. She was sure that horror movies was the topic of conversation. Jerry had met his soulmate.

Sissy never came through the line. Abby would bet her share of the gooey enchiladas she kept dipping up that Sissy had gone to the hospital. Maybe that would cheer David up. He was the lowest that Abby had ever seen him.

"I'll walk you to the library," said a voice that came from the gathering shadows. It was Martin Beecher, and it seemed he had been waiting for Abby to finish work. "How is David?"

"He'll be all right," Abby said, falling in step beside Martin. She was glad for his company.

Martin smiled at her, and she noticed how attractive he was with his unique combination of dark red hair and bright blue eyes. "Maybe we can take a break, get something to eat, after we hit the books for a while," he suggested.

"I — I'm not sure." Abby didn't want to be tied down if she saw Carrie. "I'm really tired. We spent most of last night talking to the police."

"I hadn't thought of that. Of course you did. I'll just walk you home later. I hate for you to walk back to the Quad alone after dark, what with everything that's been going on."

"Thanks for worrying." Abby smiled. She didn't want him to give up on her.

After looking up some books, she headed straight for the stacks. She was in luck. Staring at a shelf of American history books, she heard whispered arguing. She sneaked to the end of the floor-to-ceiling shelf of books. There in the next aisle was Carrie with her boyfriend, Quinton Brooks. Abby knew him only by sight and from the few remarks Carrie had made about him. But he looked angry.

Carrie whirled around and started in Abby's direction. Abby ducked back and watched her storm past. Quinton followed her, then stopped and stared, his face as dark as tornado clouds.

Abby didn't hesitate. Martin wasn't at the table, but she'd explain later where she'd gone. Grabbing her books, she jammed them into her tote.

Out on the library steps, she glanced in every direction. Carrie was practically running, but Abby spotted her disappearing into the shadows towards Varsity Pond.

Running lightly, Abby followed. She planned to stick tight to Carrie Milholland. She was going to find out where her roommate disappeared to every night.

Chapter 16

At first Abby thought Carrie was heading for the dorm. That wasn't going to answer any questions if Carrie went to their room and went to bed early.

Carrie slowed to a walk, enabling Abby to catch up. She was careful not to get too close, but Carrie never looked back. Abby waited in shadows while Carrie walked under a street lamp.

As she reached Varsity Pond, Carrie hesitated, then seemed to follow an impulse to detour into the woods. This made it easier for Abby to follow close behind. But when Carrie collapsed on a park bench and started to cry, it was all Abby could do to stay hidden, not to go sit beside her, comfort her, find out what was wrong. Well, she knew what was wrong. Carrie and Quinton were fighting.

Finally Carrie took a few ragged breaths,

blew her nose, and took a deep breath. Suddenly Abby heard her speak.

"What are you doing here?" Anger filled Carrie's voice. "You followed me, didn't you? I told you we were through."

The bench was mostly in shadow, and Abby could barely see Carrie.

She didn't recognize the low, deep voice that answered, but she was sure it was Quinton Brooks. She couldn't understand exactly what he said. The next sound was obvious. The smack of a hand on a face.

Carrie started to cry. "Stop it, Quint."

"You went to the police, didn't you?"

"Stop it! I told you I wouldn't see you again. We're through."

"I won't let you go." Another smack. He was hitting Carrie.

At last Abby understood. The bruises on Carrie's face, that's where they'd come from. Quinton Brooks had been beating up on Carrie.

The next sound was not a slap, but it was still flesh hitting flesh. Should Abby show herself? Go to help Carrie?

Of course she should. She stepped out from behind the clump of small pines and ran towards Carrie. She heard Carrie groan, down near the ground.

"Carrie, are you all right?" Abby neared the

couple. "Stop that, Quint." She called his name as if she knew him. Could she talk him out of beating up on Carrie? How could she stop this?

"Who are you?" he growled. "This is none of your business." A dark shadow loomed in front of her.

"Carrie is my roommate. You're hurting her and it isn't the first time. I'm making it my business." She addressed the voice in the darkness, the black form in front of her.

Before she could decide what to do, what else to say, Abby felt Quint's fist punch the soft flesh of her own stomach. She bent double with pain, gasping, trying to breathe.

Then she smelled the rotten odor that was so familiar. The musty, sweaty, dirty sock smells. She heard the deep, guttural growl, the moaning.

My God, it was here. Right behind her. But before she could move aside and let the monster attack Quinton Brooks — she couldn't help but hope it would — Quint punched her again.

His knuckles colliding with her chin jerked her head back, swung her around and away from Carrie on the ground.

She heard one last roar as the ground came up to meet her body slamming against it. The deepest black void of all closed around her.

Chapter 17

The first voice that penetrated her darkness was Martin's.

"Abby, Abby, are you all right? I told you I wanted to walk you home. Why didn't you listen to me? This campus isn't safe right now."

Abby felt as if her eyes were weighted with tiny sand bags. Her body was a balloon filled with lead and her legs had steel bands holding them down. But she was able to pull her lips into a tiny smile at knowing, one, she wasn't dead, and two, Martin was there, holding her in his arms.

"Oh, Abby." Maybe he saw the smile. His lips brushed hers slightly. "If you can smile, you can speak. Tell me you're all right. Whisper, I'll hear it."

"I — I'm okay, Martin," Abby whispered. "I — I — " She tried to sit up. "Keep — keep kissing me. I know that will help."

For a couple of seconds Martin's lips were warmer, firmer on hers. "Take it slowly. I'll help you." Martin pulled her to a sitting position and held her tightly in his arms. His warm body, his strength was so comforting, she wanted to stay there forever.

"Hummmmm" was all she could manage to say.

But Martin must have decided this was not the time or the place for a love scene. He changed the subject, pulling Abby back to the present. "This place reeks of that thing. Did you see it? I think it went after Quinton first. He's hurt badly, or looks as if he is. I just got a glimpse of him before the ambulance took him to the hospital."

"Carrie?" Abby whispered again.

"Scared to death, but she's all right. She's over there, talking to the police. Maybe they'll *do* something now. This person — thing — that's attacking people is definitely not carrying out a fraternity prank. Surely they know that now."

"Abby? Can you talk to us?" A strong voice came from above her. She realized it was Officer Mooney.

"I — I think so." She tried to stand and nearly fainted.

"I think she's in shock, Officer," Martin said.

"Maybe she should go to the hospital, too. Just to be sure she's all right."

"No, no, I'm fine. I just feel weak. And — and — " She remembered. "I know why my stomach hurts and my jaw feels broken. Quinton hit me. It's coming back."

"Quinton Brooks hit you?" Martin asked. "Whatever for?"

"He — he was beating up on Carrie. I got in the way. I — I had followed Carrie when she left the library. I wanted to know where she went every night. You know, Officer Mooney, because of the — the evidence on her bed. But now I know how she gets all those bruises. I learned the hard way. Quinton has been beating up on her for some time."

"Yes, Abby, we know that. She finally got up the nerve to turn him in last week. She's been staying in a safehouse. But it's hard for us to make sure a guy stays away from the girl he's abusing."

"They had a fight in the library. She left, and Quinton followed her. He started beating up on her again when she stopped by the lake."

"Why did she stop there by herself?" Martin said. "It looks as if whoever or whatever is attacking people hangs out there. You should have known that, too, Abby."

Abby's head was clearing. She must have hit

it when she fell. She groaned as she moved again, though. Her stomach still felt caved in and her jaw ached. She fought nausea.

"I — I wasn't thinking about the monster, Martin. And Carrie may not have known David was attacked here. She had other things on her mind."

"I'm going to order a full search of this area of campus," Officer Mooney said. "If the attacker is a student, he can get away easily, but he'd have to hide his costume. Maybe we can find that, or some clue to lead us to it, or him."

"Does this guy always smell like a year's supply of dirty socks?" Mooney asked.

"Yes, all musty and rotten." Abby struggled to her feet, but leaned on Martin. "Has there ever been a performance of a horror play on campus? Maybe he found a really old costume in one of the trunks in the drama department."

Maybe someone helped him find it. Her mind flew to Sissy. Maybe she helped the guy in the beginning, but when she was attracted to David, the guy got angry or jealous and hurt David to get back at Sissy.

"Good idea, Abby," Mooney said. "We'll search there, too. And your dorm. All the dorms if we have to. I'm afraid he's going to kill someone."

Abby shivered.

"You're cold, Abby." Martin took off his jacket and put it on Abby. "I'm taking her home, Officer Mooney, if that's all right with you."

"Yes, fine. We know where she is if we need any more information about tonight." Mooney turned back to where his men were aiming lights around the water. Abby realized she'd been sitting on the path above Varsity Pond, near one of the pole lights. She didn't ask how she got there.

"How'd you find me?" She did wonder about that.

"When I saw you were gone, I didn't know whether to be insulted or panicked," Martin explained. "I decided I'd go for alarm first and if you'd left with another guy, I'd deal with jealousy later."

Jealousy? Abby wondered, picking out that one word. Martin would be jealous if she left with another guy? She liked that idea. It warmed her even more than his jacket, which smelled of some earthy aftershave.

"I didn't see you anywhere when I got outside, but I guessed you might have headed for the Quad or the chem lab — I know you go there a lot when you leave the library."

"You've followed me before?" Abby accused.

"Oh, great, now you'll think I'm one of those obsessive-compulsive types. No, I didn't follow you. I overheard you say where you were going once, and then Gina told me you're there a lot, trying to raise your chem grade.

"Anyway, both the Quad and Griswold Hall are in the same direction, so I walked that way. Then I heard all that noise by the pond. By the time I got there, Carrie was hysterical. I ran to call the police. When I got back, I found Quinton looking like a disaster zone, Carrie bent over him crying. Finally I heard moaning and found you a few feet away, nearer the path. Maybe I shouldn't have moved you, but I dragged you into the light. You know the rest of the story."

"You sat by me until the police came."

"Of course. Oh, Abby, that thing could have attacked you instead of Quinton."

Abby shivered again at the idea. But she started to feel angry, too. If Quinton hadn't punched her out, she might have been able to see the monster, get some idea of what it looked like and maybe even identify who it was.

"Come on, Abby," Martin urged. "I'm taking you to your room. You're going to feel worse tomorrow. And you may look like a Saturday night brawl." He laughed a little.

"I don't know why men like fighting each other." Abby rubbed her jaw again. "Getting punched out hurts."

"Most of us don't like to fight. But it comes in handy to know how. Haven't you ever been insulted, or so angry you felt like hitting someone?"

"I guess I can understand a little. I wanted to hit Quinton when he hit Carrie. But all I did was yell at him. And get in his way. That wasn't very effective, was it?"

"Abby, could Carrie have been carrying a knife?" Martin asked, his tone sober.

"You mean, she could have gotten angry enough to cut Quinton?"

"Women have been known to fight back. Eventually. When they're pushed too far. Maybe when he hit you, her friend — "

"But that wouldn't explain why this whole place smells like the monster."

"I guess you're right." Martin took Abby's arm.

A crowd had gathered at the other end of the path, under the other light. As Abby and Martin approached it, people began to murmur. "Are you all right, Abby?" someone asked.

She nodded as she looked up to see who had asked. It was Jess. "Yes, I'll be okay. Thanks."

Before she looked back at the path, having

to think about every weary step, she saw someone else staring at her.

Stan Hurley stood at one end of the crowd,
his eyes glued to hers. She couldn't read his
expression, but goose bumps rose on her arms
again at seeing him here.

It seemed like too much of a coincidence to
think he'd just happened along like everyone
else had. Then hung around to find out what
was happening.

And then Abby saw an eerie smile flit over
his lips.

Chapter 18

Abby worked really hard in chem lab the next day so she wouldn't have to work at night. There was hardly a night that she came in the lab that Stan Hurley wasn't there. She didn't want to be alone with him.

Her extra credit experiment was almost finished — again. She'd found it difficult to remember her initial conception of the project — and she had to admit, the first experiment was partly an accident. A lot of famous discoveries were accidents, weren't they? She wished David were here. He was such a genius in chemistry. Maybe she'd cut her class before lunch and go see him. The bandages were coming off today. He would need support.

She did just that. On the way, she stopped at Burgers Etc., the long, silver diner midway between campus and town. She knew David would be ready for some real food by now.

Coke in hand, she slipped into his room, wanting to surprise him. Just as she opened her mouth to say, "Surprise!" she caught a glimpse of David's face. The Coke dropped from her hand, liquid and ice spilling around him on the bed at the same time a gasp escaped her mouth. "Oh!"

David's eyes had been closed, but he wasn't asleep. He raised up on one elbow and stared at her as if she were a total stranger. Then he went limp, turned his face away, and stared out the window.

"Pretty bad, isn't it?"

"I — it'll be better when the scratches heal." What else could she say now that she had made a scene as well as a mess? "I've made a terrible mess." She hurried to scoop up ice in her empty cup. "Let's ring for the nurse and get you another sheet."

"Ask for a new face at the same time, will you?"

"Oh, David." Abby sat on the chair by his bed instead of continuing her cleanup. "I'm so sorry. But no kidding, when the scratches heal, you'll probably only have tiny scars."

"Yeah, sure."

The stitches and welts created angry hot pink designs on what had once been the most handsome face Abby had ever seen outside of the movies. David could have been a model or a movie star if he wanted to.

Think fast, Abby, she ordered her brain. "I brought you a burger from Burgers Etc. And fries, too. Here, sit up. If the nurse comes in, she'll take it away from you. There's a rule that hospital patients can only have carrot mush and green Jell-O." Rattling the bag, she spread out David's picnic.

"I'll eat if you'll stop pretending, Abby." Slowly, David sat up, looked in the white paper bag. "No ketchup?"

"At the bottom of the fries. They may be soggy, but think what'll be on the hospital lunch tray."

Abby sat for a few seconds, unwrapping the silver paper from her own burger. The greasy smell filled her nostrils, making her stomach churn. She took a bite anyway, chewed slowly.

"Okay, you look awful. Have you considered plastic surgery?"

"The doctor wants to wait and see. Maybe I'll grow a beard. And a mustache. And my bangs long." David's attempt at humor was lame. "This food is wonderful, Abby. Thanks."

"Has Sissy been in?"

"Yes. I asked her not to come back. I can't stand the way she looks at me."

"She'll be all right. It's just that the initial shock is — is — "

"Yeah. I hope my mother won't come. She'll make a scene."

Abby didn't know what else to say. The silence became awkward. "I guess I'd better get back to school. I cut my English lit class, but I don't dare cut history."

"Abby," David took her hand. His brown eyes looked concerned. "Don't walk across the campus by yourself at night until this thing is caught."

Abby hadn't told David about Quinton Brooks punching her out. Or his being attacked. She figured he'd hear soon enough, and she didn't want him to worry about her. She'd carefully covered her bruises with makeup, and he apparently hadn't noticed them.

"I've decided for sure it's Stan Hurley doing this, David." She needed to talk to someone. "I don't know why, or even how he's doing it. The police are looking for a costume. But I don't have any proof. He acts like he's angry at the whole world. He may have attacked you simply because you — you're so good-looking." She almost said "were." He would be again, she hoped.

"People don't just start attacking other people because they're angry."

"Yes, they do. You read about it all the time. Someone takes a gun into McDonald's and shoots total strangers because a love affair broke up. Some man shot up the post office because he got fired."

"Those people are already disturbed, psychotic."

"Stan Hurley is disturbed, and weird besides." Abby had made up her mind. Now she only had to prove it.

"I've got to run." She leaned over and kissed David. "Get well, and try not to worry about losing your handsome dude status. I'll come back soon."

Not only was she clumsy physically, spilling that Coke all over David, but she left feeling everything she'd said to make him feel better was clumsy. But what could you say to someone whose face looked like barbed wire tracks? And David's eyes hadn't been damaged. He could see for himself how he looked.

Stan couldn't possibly have hurt David because he was her boyfriend, could he? Out of jealousy? She had never given Stan Hurley any encouragement. If he liked her, she couldn't do anything about it. When did liking someone turn into obsession?

A plan started to take shape in her mind. It was probably a dumb thing to do, but for some reason she felt partly responsible for Stan's behavior. She'd hide and follow him tonight. She knew he'd be at the lab. He was there every night. He left after she did — and maybe he followed her. Maybe he'd followed her last night and when Quinton punched her out, it made Stan angry. He'd attacked Quinton.

Well, if Stan was following her, she'd turn the tables on him. At least she'd feel like she was *doing* something.

"Want to study together tonight, Abby?" Martin asked, stopping her later, after class.

"No, I — I have something else I have to do." Her vagueness brought a question to Martin's eyes. She hurried to answer it. "It's important, Martin, but I can't tell you about it. Don't take this personally."

He did, but he tried to be nice about it. "You went to see David, didn't you?"

"Yes. He needs me right now, Martin. I'm sorry."

"It's all right. You're a giving person, Abby. But don't be a martyr. David wasn't exactly thoughtful of you before this happened."

Stress was getting to Abby. She took it out on Martin. "I think that's my business, Martin. Don't try to tell me what to do."

"I wouldn't think of it." Martin said, biting

off his words. Then he spun around abruptly and walked away from Abby. She'd never seen him so angry.

Abby watched him go. Why was everything that was happening today going against her? She liked Martin. And David had been breaking up with her for Sissy. Why did she feel so guilty over all this?

Control, Abby. You're a control freak, remember? She heard her best friend's voice from high school. She wished Carol were here right now. She could sure use a best friend to talk to.

Carol was brutally honest, like a best friend should be. Abby knew she liked being in control of her life. She liked order, too. She liked straight A's, being on the honor roll, handing in all her work on time. Keeping her room clean. She liked working at the Quad Caf, wiping tables, filling salt shakers.

She sighed and sank onto a bench in the Commons. She wanted David to be the way he was again. Then she wouldn't feel guilty breaking up with him, even though he was the one running after Sissy. She had wanted to protect Carrie from an abusive boyfriend last night. *Who are you to think you can set the world in order, Abby, keep bad things from happening, fix them when they do?*

Carol's voice echoed inside her head again. *Who are you to think you can catch this beast thing when the police can't?*

It could be dangerous.

But that was exactly what she was going to do.

Tonight.

Chapter 19

If Stan was nothing else, he was predictable. About nine o'clock, to be sure she didn't miss him, Abby dressed in black and waited in the bushes beside Griswold Hall. As late as it was in the spring, it should have been warm, but it wasn't. Rain had started to fall right after dinner. It had settled now to a cool mist and the dampness sank right through her warm-up suit, through her long-sleeved black T-shirt, and into her skin. In no time, she started shivering.

Right after ten, according to the luminous dial of her watch, Abby saw the familiar husky shape walk out of the front entrance. He wore a backpack, and in the dark he looked like the Hunchback of Notre Dame.

Stan glanced both ways, then started in the direction of Varsity Pond. Keeping to the shadows, Abby followed.

He carried a flashlight, so it wasn't hard to keep up. He entered the woods and started looking around. It appeared he was searching for something.

Had he dropped something last night that would implicate him? He'd missed it today and figured it must be at the scene of his last crime?

Wind rustled the pines around the pond making them sigh and whisper. Abby glanced around, suddenly sure someone was in the woods besides her and Stan.

She saw no one.

But it was so dark, how could she tell?

She let herself be distracted for so long, she almost missed Stan leaving the pond and starting up the hill on the path west of the small grove of trees.

Hurrying to keep up yet stay hidden, she slipped on the wet grassy slope and thudded to her knees. She scrambled to her feet, limping a little until the pain went out of her left knee, and padded up the trail. At the top she slowed, stayed in the bushes, and peeked out. Stan was way ahead of her. But someone was on the path behind her.

She slipped farther into the underbrush and squatted down. Drops of water showered her, making her wetter than ever. Why hadn't she worn a windbreaker or her poncho? Because your poncho is bright yellow, she remembered.

A couple passed her, arm in arm, sharing an umbrella, talking quietly. She waited a couple of seconds for them to get ahead, then stepped back onto the path.

Where was Stan? She practically ran so she wouldn't lose him, pretending to be a jogger, passing the couple now that she knew if they saw her it wouldn't matter.

In no time, she was breathing heavily, practically gasping for air. She wasn't a jogger. She never wanted to be. But she gained the grounds of Abbey House just in time to see a shadow that had to be Stan slip around behind it.

Cutting across the lawn, she walked fast. She was gasping for air so loudly she felt she might as well yell, I'm here behind you. But Stan didn't turn around.

She realized Stan was heading for the ruins of Peabody Gym. Why was he going there? The only connection she could make was that it was another place where the beast had been seen, where it had made its first appearance.

By the time she got to the burned hulk, she remembered the story. Cheerleaders dying in a wreck, people dying in the fire — the memory didn't improve her mood.

Where was Stan? A light flashed at a corner

of the ruin. There. She slipped through a patch of wet weeds and into the shadows. Peering carefully around the half wall, she could see enough to know Stan was searching here, too. She didn't know what she had hoped to find out by following him, but she hadn't expected him to be looking around in every place the monster had appeared.

What did that mean? Her best idea was still that Stan had lost something on one of his night adventures and needed it back, something that would say Stan Hurley was here. He's the one turning into a fearful beast that attacks when he feels like it.

The sneeze came on without any warning. Even so, Abby tried to contain it, but the muffled blast of air sounded like a rifle shot to her. She crouched and huddled close to the rough wall, which smelled of earth and scorched wood.

What would Stan say or do if he caught her following him? How did he turn into the beast? If he did so at will, or if anger made him change, would he hunt down whoever was following him and attack? If he needed the costume, did he have it with him? In that backpack he carried? Would he change into it to disguise himself and then find her?

She tried to make her body into an even

smaller ball, hoping her dark clothing would keep her hidden. Expecting a light shining in her eyes in any moment, she hugged her legs tight to her chest and waited. He could hear her heart pounding, couldn't he? It thudded until it reached her temples where it pulsed, making her feel lightheaded and faint. She couldn't pass out. She forced herself to concentrate on keeping alert.

Think of a story. Think of a reason for being hidden here. If Stan found her, she could always say she had come out there to get a breath of fresh air. That she always walked at night when she needed to wake up and study for a few hours longer. It didn't matter that now it was really raining. She loved walking in the rain.

Then why aren't you walking? I — I stopped here to rest a minute. Oh, this was getting ridiculous. Uncurling, she stood up. Then she peeked back around the wall. She saw nothing. No light, no Stan Hurley, nothing but rain streaming down her face, hair stringing in her eyes.

So much for being a private detective.

Wetter than she'd ever been in her life — at least when wearing clothes and not a bathing suit — she sloshed across the field and towards the Quad. The people in the lobby looked at her as if she had three heads.

Carrie stared as she pushed open the door to their room and stood for a second dripping. "Abby, you're wet."

The understatement of the year. "Get me a towel, will you, Carrie?"

Abby buried her face in the fresh scent of the thick, soft, terry cloth. She felt so foolish. And miserable. She sneezed again. She and Carrie still hadn't really talked about what had happened with Quint, but that was the last thing on Abby's mind now.

"Let me help you get those clothes off, Abby." Carrie tugged at the T-shirt sleeves that had become a second skin. She peeled Abby's jeans off where they wanted to stick tight to her legs. "You're going to be sick."

It was a good prediction. For three days she stayed in bed with a terrible head cold. It was the only thing she caught while chasing after Stan Hurley.

Carrie brought her soup and juice. Gina and Jerry brought her aspirin and decongestant. There was a three-day lull in Abby's life.

But late on Thursday afternoon, she awoke dreaming she was falling, falling, failing . . . failing chemistry!

She sat straight up in bed. Oh my gosh, her extra-credit report was due the next day, Friday. Without it she wouldn't fail, but she definitely wouldn't get a decent grade.

Struggling to her feet, weak from lying in bed for three days, she pulled on the only close-to-clean clothes she could find. The thick, woolly sweatshirt felt good.

After a few minutes she realized she didn't feel too bad. She had caught up on her sleep, shut out the world for a short time. Was it all due to her being sick? No, she had needed to escape. She blew her nose, ignoring how raw and sore it felt, popped a couple more aspirin, and gathered her chem book and her lab notebook.

Carrie wasn't in the room. She had mothered Abby for these three days, but wasn't there now to say, "Don't go out. You shouldn't get out of bed yet."

The rain was over. The evening was warm and smelled of lilacs and honeysuckle. Abby was pleased that she could smell them. And she didn't feel bad at all. If she could get her report finished quickly, maybe she'd see if any place was open and get something besides soup to eat. She felt starved.

Closer to Varsity Pond, the safe feeling she'd

had curled in her bed started to seep away. A crunch of gravel behind her caused her to swing around and see who was behind her. No one.

It was awfully dark, so she stayed on the lighted paths. But taking the shortcut to Griswold Hall was too tempting. It was only a few yards across the grass and around the grove of trees by the lake. People had made such a habit of taking this route, a dirt path was cut into the lawn.

On her left, in the woods, leaves rustled. She hurried even more, trying to see into the shadows. A limb cracked as if someone had stepped on it. How could she have forgotten about the beast?

She ran, expecting to feel hot breath at her back. She dashed into the lighted area ahead, looking back just to make sure.

Ooof! She collided with someone. Her book and notebook flew from her hands. Her purse bounced, popped open, spilled its guts on the walk.

"Hey, watch where you're going." A guy she didn't know grasped both her arms, keeping her from falling.

"Oh, I'm sorry. I'm so sorry. I — I — "

He took a better look at her. "Well, maybe I don't mind your running into me after all.

Why haven't I noticed you before?"

This was not the time or the place to flirt with anyone.

"I'm really sorry." Abby started picking up things and placing them back in her purse. He helped. "Please, you don't have to help me. I'm — I'm just clumsy."

He stood looking down at her. "Nice running into you anyway." He left her alone.

She reached the lab with no further incident and was relieved to find it empty. Placing her book and notebook on the counter beside her station, she paged through the notebook, the paper crackling in the stillness. Where was her special project page? Impatience made her page through the book furiously.

It took a few minutes for her to focus and calm down. Finally she found what she was looking for, bent the other pages around the spiral so only the list of chemicals she needed lay in front of her. She walked to her locker, spun the dial on the lock, got out her apron, and tied it on.

She got out a mortar bowl, stared at the list of chemicals again. Three days away made her feel strange here, as if this were a foreign land and she didn't belong, didn't speak the language. Gathering the chemicals, walking back and forth, lining them up before her, helped her slip into a routine.

Soon she lost all sense of time and the feeling of not belonging. She perched on her stool, measured and added each ingredient. Then, almost down to the last vial on her list, she froze, measuring spoon in midair.

She was no longer alone. Someone stood behind her.

A low voice said, "I thought you might be back tonight. Where have you been? I've missed you."

Chapter 20

"What are you doing here?" Abby backed away.

"The same as you, working on extra-credit projects." Stan laughed. "Why are you so surprised? Or disturbed by the idea that I'm here? You've been following me around, haven't you? Well, here I am." He held out both arms as if to hug her. His grin made her shudder. "For someone who wouldn't go out with me, you've certainly paid me a lot of attention."

She stepped back again. "That's not true." It was, but she wasn't going to admit it. "You've been following me. Every time I look up, there you are."

"You could say you've been the center of attention in several recent strange and disturbing circumstances. Anyone would be fascinated by your behavior."

What could she answer to that? Stan was

right. "If someone was attacking all your friends, you'd be concerned, too."

"True. I guess I would. But as you may have observed, I don't have a huge following of friends. I prefer it that way, however. I like being left alone. And I would appreciate your doing that in the future." Stan moved towards his table.

The nerve. He was telling *her* to leave *him* alone. She wasn't going to let him walk away. "What project are you working on?"

"I don't think you'd understand it if I told you."

Anger replaced fear inside of Abby. The hand still holding the quarter teaspoon of chemicals shook until she dumped it into the brew she was mixing.

It took her three tries to ignite a match and light her Bunsen burner. The small jet of gas roared to life. She placed the dish over the flame and stumbled over her stool as she hurried to get the last ingredient. At least she was close to the mixture she had spoiled once and had had trouble duplicating.

Keeping her eyes on her own experiment, she tried to forget that Stan was on the other side of the room. But since only the two stations were lit, it was hard to ignore the glow of his lamp. She couldn't avoid seeing him hunched over his counter, his hair sticking up in all directions, his glasses slipping down his nose, a frown on his face as he concentrated. He had certainly forgotten her.

Twice she glanced up. He was totally immersed in his work.

Her nerves kept her pacing. She stopped at the water fountain and let the cold water splash her cheeks, her forehead, her lips. Then she drank deeply. Wiping her face with the bottom of her apron, she noticed the odor starting to fill the room.

God, what was Stan cooking up? The smell was awful. Rotten, musty. She hurried back to her own mixture, which had started to bubble. The smell — the rotten smell — it wasn't from Stan's side of the room. The fumes came from the mess she was heating.

Quickly she flicked off the burner. A tiny memory flirted with her mind. The smell, this was the way it had smelled the day she spilled it. At least she knew she had matched that mixture.

With a padded glove she slid the dish off the burner onto a hot pad. At the same time a strange sensation crept over her. She felt slightly dizzy from the fumes. She leaned on the stool, slid the glove off, gripped the counter with both hands.

She stared, unbelieving. Her hands were sprouting coarse hair all across the back. Up and down the tops of her fingers.

Her fingers swelled slightly, bent at the joints. Her fingernails were growing longer, curving into razor-sharp claws.

A musty smell surrounded her.

Finally what was happening registered in her mind.

She — she —

Her scream echoed off the walls of the cavernous room.

Chapter 21

"Oh, my God, it's me. It's me that's the monster! Stan, help! Help me!" Abby backed away from the rotten smelling mixture on the counter.

Her stomach churned with nausea and anger. Anger! She needed to lash out against something, someone. The strength to do so swelled within her. A sense of power surrounded her, filled her. Her face stretched and contorted with her rage.

Stan was at her side immediately. His image blurred before her. "Abby, my God," he whispered. "I was right."

"Stan, help me, help me, Stan. Please, please, help me."

"What did you mix up, Abby? Did you drink it? Taste it at all?"

"No, no, of course not. I — I — can't remember."

"You have to remember. I can't help you unless I know what you did to cause this. What gave off that smell?"

"The smell. It was that stuff." It was all she could do to control her rage, the urge to attack Stan. She struggled to stay Abby. Something else wanted to get out, was getting out. Fight, Abby, fight, she told herself.

"You breathed the fumes?"

"Yes. I — I couldn't help it. When it started boiling, I — "

Stan grabbed the now cooled dish and dumped its contents down the sink. "What was in it, Abby? What ingredients? In what proportions?" Stan shook her.

She reached for him. He had no right to touch her, to shake her. She'd kill him.

"Fight it, Abby, fight. Keep it away until you've told me."

"It's — it's in my notebook."

"Your lab notebook?"

"In . . . in the back . . . last page." Abby was losing. Waves of dizziness washed over her. She clutched her face with both . . . both paws. It felt misshapen. Her mouth had stretched. Her teeth were long and sharp.

She moaned, groaned, then roared. The sound filled the room, bounced back at her, caused her to roar again.

"I'm sorry to do this, Abby."

Stan whirled her around, ducking her swinging claws. He pushed with all his strength. Abby stumbled towards the large closet that held extra equipment and chemicals.

She fell into the darkness and immediately spun around and growled. Doubled up, rose to her knees, swung her claws. A door slammed in her face and she raked it, digging deep into the soft wood panels.

She stood, pounded, pushed with all her strength. She must get out. She must attack whoever had locked her into this darkness. This small space that contained her. She would not be contained. Kill — kill him. She would kill him.

Anger turned her mind to hot lava, spilling over, spinning her around. One paw raked glass beakers onto the floor. Another ripped the shelf from the wall. She threw it into another wall of jars and bottles.

Again and again she pounded on the door. She felt it give slightly. She pushed with all her weight. The door was flimsy. She was strong, so strong, so angry, so powerful. She would not be stopped by a slab of wood. She slammed her fist into the top panel. The wood shattered. She kicked at the bottom. Her foot shot through the panel, splintering it.

One more deep, satisfying roar vibrated around her. She raised both powerful arms, crashed through the door, flinging it aside like cardboard. She loved the sound.

There he was. Her victim. She stumbled towards him.

"Get back, Abby. I need — I need one more minute." Stan backed away from her. She followed. He snapped a switch that threw on all the lights in the room.

"There! I think I have it. Pray it works, Abby. For you and for me." Stan threw a glass vial at her.

She hated the light, shielded her eyes. At the same time, she laughed, shrieked, roared again. He thought that small tube of glass could stop her. She reached for him as acrid fumes surrounded her. Coughing, she grasped both of his arms, started to lift him up, slam him against the wall.

Then — then — she sank into a deep black void. Down, down, down she fell, her mind in darkness.

Until a black hole consumed her, held her captive.

Chapter 22

"Let me go! Let go!" Abby struggled to get out of Stan's arms. "What do you mean? What are you doing? Get away from me."

Abby scooted away from Stan, then realized she was sitting in something that smelled awful. Almost as bad as — as —

She began to remember.

She broke into uncontrollable sobbing, a hysterical crying jag that lasted for several minutes. Stan let her cry. He crouched beside her.

Slowly, slowly her control was returning. She felt so empty, so frightened, so alone.

"It was me, Stan. I was that — that thing. I attacked people, hurting them. David — I did that to David." She sobbed again.

Stan circled her with both his strong arms. Pulled her close and held her tightly until she stopped crying. Then he pulled out a huge white handkerchief and handed it to her.

She mopped her face, blew her nose. "How could I? How could I do such a thing?"

"It wasn't *you*, Abby. It was what you turned into."

"But I — I didn't want to turn into that — that thing. It was that stuff I mixed up, wasn't it? That awful smell."

"Yes, you did something pretty remarkable when you come right down to it." Stan talked as she struggled to calm down. "I've always wondered what Dr. Jekyll mixed up and drank to turn into Mr. Hyde. You discovered it, or something similar. You've made some kind of chemical breakthrough. By accident."

"Oh, Stan, I didn't mean to. And I hurt people. Look at all the people I hurt."

"But the miracle of it." Stan's voice held awe.

"I — I don't want some kind of Nobel prize for chemistry, Stan. I just want this to be a terrible nightmare. To wake up and find I dreamed it."

"That's not going to happen."

"What can I do?" Abby started thinking about David again. "Poor David. The scars. He's going to have awful scars because of me. Why did I do that to him, when I was that — that terrible beast?"

"Well, I have two theories, Abby." Stan scooted away from Abby now that she was calm. He crossed his legs and hugged his knees, as if this were some kind of normal philosophical discussion they were having. "The first attacks were random. You attacked Lenny because he was there when the first spell hit you. I guess the reaction was delayed the first few times it happened. Then it became easier to change."

"And Jerry. I must have left here and once I — I changed, I wandered into those woods. He came along . . ."

"Then David made you angry. It was becoming easier for you to make the transformation. You were reexposed to the chemicals each time you tried to mix up that brew again. So it became easier and easier to change. I think anger triggered the appearance of the beast the last two times."

"I wasn't angry enough to hurt David." Abby bit her lip to keep from crying again.

"Sometimes we don't realize how much anger is stored inside of us, Abby. My theory is that you've always been a very nice girl. And a control freak. There must have been many times over the years when you've suppressed anger, pushed it down, said I will stay in control, not lose my temper."

"You're right. I've done that. I tried not to

be angry at Sissy, at David. I tried to be a good sport, Stan."

"I'm not much of one to preach, Abby. I keep a lot of anger inside myself, too. But there's nothing like a huge yelling, screaming fit of temper to clear the air. Anger itself is a nasty beast if it's not let out occasionally."

"But look at what I've done. I have to accept responsibility."

"Yes, you do. But I'd have to say that Quinton Brooks deserved being attacked. Men who beat up on women are the worst kind of animals."

Abby's first apology was to Stan. "You know, Stan, you're not as bad a guy as I thought you were. How can I ever thank you for tonight? What would I have done if you hadn't been there?"

"I don't know. But acknowledge my genius at finding an antidote for your potion so fast," Stan grinned.

"You can have my chemistry award, Stan. How'd you do that?"

"To tell the truth, Abby, I've suspected you for a while now. And so I followed you, to see if my hypothesis was accurate. I had already given some thought to what you might have mixed up and what might counteract it. If I hadn't hit on the right mixture, you would have put me in the hospital tonight."

Abby studied her hands, her back-to-normal hands. Surely this was all a dream, a nightmare. Again she wished it were. She got to her feet, looked around. The storage closet was a shambles. It was no dream. *She* had done that. She picked up her notebook, stained with a yellowish-brown color. Flipped to the last page of notes.

"I have to call the police, Stan. I have to turn myself in. I don't know what they'll do, but — "

"There probably isn't any precedent for this kind of case, unless you count the novel, but Hyde killed his victims."

"What if the police don't believe me?"

"I guess you can just write it off to experience, forget about it, since it won't happen again."

"I can't forget this, Stan."

"I know you can't, Abby. But I do have one suggestion before you do anything else."

"What's that?"

"This formula, list of chemicals and proportions — "

"Should be destroyed. You're right." Abby ripped the sheet from her notebook. The flame still burned on her Bunsen burner. She held the paper sideways over the fire. Watched as it flamed, burned down to ashes. She crumbled the ashes on the counter.

She walked to Dr. Curruthers's office. The wooden door she — no, *the monster* — had thrown had broken the glass in the office door. She reached in, turned the lock, opened it. Stan followed her inside. She rested her hand on the phone for a few seconds.

"Will I have to leave Salem?"

"It depends. Maybe the police will agree to keep this whole thing secret."

"I can't think right now what would be the best for everyone concerned." Abby couldn't even imagine telling Officer Mooney her story. She started to dial 911.

Stan's hand covered hers. "Abby, I know I'm not much in the social graces department. I've never even dated a girl before." He held up one hand as she looked at him, eyes wide. "Hey, I'm not asking again for you to go out with me. But you're going to need a friend. One who does believe what's happened. If you'd let me — if — "

"I'd be honored, Stan. Thanks. You might turn out to be the best friend I've ever had."

Abby reached for the phone again to report — to turn in the monster that had been terrorizing Salem University.

*They sat in a circle around the blazing fire,
their features distorted by the dancing orange
and yellow flames. Their heads were down,
their jackets pulled tightly around them for
warmth.*

They called themselves The Others.

*Norman dropped to a crouching position.
The firelight played across his thin, pale face,
casting eerie shadows that turned his skin to
reddish-orange and lit a menacing yellow light
in his eyes.*

*Thunder sounded in the distance, and an
ominous black cloud swept across the half
moon overhead. An owl hooted a question; bat
wings fluttered in the tall, black trees.*

Someone giggled nervously.

*Molly studied the way the dancing flames
seemed to change Norman's bone structure.
His face reminded her now of a tall, narrow*

jack-o'-lantern her grandfather had once carved on Halloween. She'd been upset because pumpkins were supposed to be round, and this one wasn't. "You can't make a jack-o'-lantern out of that skinny thing!" she had cried.

But he had. And thanks to his cleverness with the knife, the resulting work of art had been the scariest Molly had ever seen. Its mouth opened as if in a scream. Its crooked, pointed teeth, its slanted, narrow eyes, had looked far more sinister than any round pumpkin could.

That was how Norman's face looked now as he began to explain the purpose behind The Others. His face seemed sinister, menacing . . . An optical illusion, of course, created by the wavering yellow and red flames.

Of course . . .

"And now for our initiation," Norman said, rising to his feet.

They all rose with him.

About the Author

"Writing tales of horror makes it hard to convince people that I'm a nice, gentle person," says **Diane Hoh.**

"So what's a nice woman like me doing scaring people?

"Discovering the fearful side of life: what makes the heart pound, the adrenaline flow, the breath catch in the throat. And hoping always that the reader is having a frightfully good time, too."

Diane Hoh grew up in Warren, Pennsylvania. Since then, she has lived in New York, Colorado, and North Carolina, before settling in Austin, Texas. "Reading and writing take up most of my life," says Hoh, "along with family, music, and gardening." Her other horror novels include *Funhouse*, *The Accident*, *The Invitation*, *The Fever*, and *The Train*.

NIGHTMARE HALL

where college is a scream!